Disfigured Love

Georgia Le Carre

D1341530

Cover design: www.EstrellaCoverArt.com Viola Estrella cover
designer
Editor: http://www.loriheaford.com/
Proofreader: http://nicolarhead.wix.com/editingservices

Disfigured Love

Published by Georgia Le Carre
Copyright © 2014 by Georgia Le Carre

ISBN: 978-0-9929969-0-1

You can discover more information about Georgia
Le Carre and future releases here.
https://www.facebook.com/georgia.lecarre
https://twitter.com/georgiaLeCarre
http://www.goodreads.com/GeorgiaLeCarre

ALSO BY GEORGIA

The Billionaire Banker Series
Owned
42 Days
Besotted
Seduce Me
Love's Sacrifice

Masquerade

Pretty Wicked
(Novella)

Click on the link below to receive news of my
latest releases, fabulous giveaways, and
exclusive content.
http://bit.ly/1oe9WdE

This book is dedicated to
Nichole Hart and Cariad of
http://www.sizzlingpages.com
These two beautiful women let me stand on
their shoulders to get here.

They must have the forbidden fruit, or paradise
will not be paradise for them.

—Alexander Pushkin, *Eugene Onegin*

Table of Contents

Once upon a time...

there lived a...

Hawke

Her eyes are a mutation. A beautiful
mutation.

It was late when I finally stopped working
and reached for the red envelope laid at the
edge of the desk. I placed it in front of me,
and simply stared at it, as if it held some great
and frightening secret. In fact, its contents
were prosaic and vulgar.

Some months ago, late one night, I had
become so unbearably lonely and unhappy
that I had actually *craved* the forgiving curves
of a woman—any woman. So I went on the
dark net, a place where all depravity is catered
for and anything one could possibly wish for
is in ready supply. I found myself a
procurement agency... And signed up. In that
brief moment I became everything I had
detested in other men.

The intolerable loneliness of that fateful
night no longer possessed me, but ever since
then a red envelope had arrived once every

two weeks. I'll admit, I did open the envelopes and look at the photos of those poor girls, modern day sex slaves. But even though each one was exquisitely beautiful, not once had I been even slightly tempted. I skimmed their fresh faces and nubile bodies without interest, sometimes with regret at my lapse in judgment, and other times marveling at the extent of my need. Never in my life had I paid for a woman and certainly not for an unwilling one.

I didn't even know why I still looked. Curiosity? Compulsion? But each time I stuffed those photos back into the envelope and threw them away, I became the unforgivable beast who condemned them to a fate worse than death.

With a sigh I tore the envelope open and slid the photographs out. My eyes widened. What the fuck! I began to shake uncontrollably. The photographs fell from my nerveless hands and landed on my desk with a soft hiss.

This girl had cast her eyes out and looked *back* at me.

In a daze I picked up the photo and stared at her...ravenously. At her enormous translucent gray eyes, the small, perfectly formed nose, the flawlessly pale skin, the long lustrous blonde hair that spilled out and lay in curves around her full lips and slender neck.

There was something clean and 'new' about her, as if she had just come out of tissue

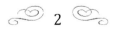

paper. I reached for the other photo. Wearing a black bikini and red high heels, her arms at her sides, she stood in a bare room, the same one all the other girls had stood in. Leggy. Shining. Unlucky.

I turned the photo over.

Lena Seagull.

The bitter irony of it did not escape me. The hawk's prey is the seagull, after all. Her age and vital statistics were displayed in English, French, Arabic and Chinese. I let my eyes skim over them, although they were no longer of any importance. To my shock and horror I couldn't walk away from this one. No. Not this one.

Age: 18
Status: Certified Virgin
Height: 5'9"
Dress Size: 6-8-10
Bust: 34"
Waist: 24"
Hips: 35.5"
Shoe Size: 7
Hair: Blonde
Eyes: Dove Gray
Languages: Russian and English

My hand shook as my fingers traced the unsmiling outline of her beautiful face. How strange, but I yearned for the smell of her skin, the taste of those plump lips. I had never known such irresistible desire before. I wanted her so bad it hurt. At that moment of longing I felt it, as if the photo was alive; I had an impression of a quiet, but terrible grief.

I snatched my hand away, as if burnt, and frowned at the photo. I must not fall under her spell. And yet, wasn't it already too late? The connection was instantaneous, beyond my control. I felt desperate to acquire her, brand her with my body. And make her mine. I turned to my computer screen and tapped in the secret code. The encrypted message was only one word long.

YES.

Almost instantly my phone rang. I snatched it and pressed the receiver to my ear.

'The auction will be held at two p.m. Friday,' a man's voice said in an Eastern European accent. 'And,' he continued, 'I must warn you. She will not be cheap. I believe there are already two Arab princes who are also interested. What's your limit?'

'None,' I said instantly. In my mind she was already mine.

A pause. Then, '*Very* good.'

I terminated the call. There, it was done. I had sealed both our fates. My eyes seeking hers fell upon my own disfigured hand. Claw-like and ugly. And I heard again, as if it had

happened yesterday, the sickeningly angry screech of metal against metal, the explosion that had strangely brought with it a blissful silence, and then the bitter smell of my own flesh burning, burning, burning: watching my skin bubble, crackle, glow and smoke. I had sizzled and cooked like a piece of steak on a fucking barbecue. I thought of the shimmering waves that rose from my flesh and shuddered.

My good hand moved upwards and stroked the raised scars on my face. The truth yawned like a black mouth: she would *never* come to love me. I was no longer fit for love. A beauty such as she was stardust. I was destined only for the part of the lovestruck fool clutching vainly for the hem of her skirt as she blazed past. My hand jerked with the sudden pain blooming in my chest. It ate like acid. It was so horrendous that tears filled my eyes and a howl escaped from my mouth. The sound vibrated and echoed around the cavernous room like the cry of a wounded beast.

The sound shocked and disgusted me. I had never been weak. And I was not about to start now. I hardened my heart.

And so fucking what if she would never come to know my heart? I would have her, anyway. And think no more of it. She would be my pet. A human pet. To do with as I pleased. I laughed out loud. The sound rang out in the stillness. Unlike the sound of my anguish, which had throbbed with vital life, my laughter was empty and soulless. It disappeared into that deathly quiet castle and went to lie softly on my two secrets as they lay unconscious to the world.

Chapter 1

Lena Seagull

My name is not really Lena Seagull. Seagull is the nickname my father was given by those who knew him. While you were alive he would steal everything from you, and when you were dead he would steal even your eyeballs.

My first vivid memory is one of violence.

I was not yet five years old and I had disobeyed my father. I had refused to do something he wanted me to. I cannot remember what it was anymore, but it was something small and insignificant. Definitely unimportant. He did not get angry, he just nodded thoughtfully. He turned toward my mother. 'Catherine,' he said calmly. 'Put a pot of water on to boil.'

I remember my mother's white face and her frightened eyes clearly. She knew my father, you see. She hung a pot of water on the open fire of the stove.

He sat and smoked his pipe quietly. Behind me my sisters and brother huddled. There were seven of us then. I was the youngest. Two more would come after me.

'Has the water boiled yet?' my father asked every so often.

'No,' she said, her voice trembling with fear, and he nodded and carried on puffing on his pipe.

Eventually, she said, 'Yes. The water is ready.'

Two of my sisters began to sob quietly. My father carefully put his pipe down on the table and stood.

'Come here,' he called to my mother. There was no anger. Perhaps he even sighed.

But by now my mother's fear had communicated itself to me and I had begun to fidget, fret and hop from foot to foot in abject terror. I sobbed and cried out, 'I'm sorry. I'm very sorry. I will never again do such a thing.'

My father ignored me.

'Please, please, Papa,' I begged.

'Put the child on the chair,' he instructed.

My mother, with tears streaming down her cheeks, put me on the chair. Even then I think she already knew exactly what was about to happen because she smiled at me sadly, but with such love that I remember it to this day.

I stood up and clung desperately to my mother's legs. My father ordered my older sisters to hold me down. They obeyed him immediately.

Reluctantly, my mother dragged her feet back to my father.

With the dizzying speed of a striking snake he grabbed her hand and plunged it into the boiling water. My mother's eyes bulged and she opened her mouth to scream, but the only sound that came out was the choke that someone makes when they are trying to vomit. While she writhed and twisted like a cut snake in his grip, my father turned his beautiful eyes toward me. My father was an extremely handsome man—laughing gray eyes and blond hair.

The shock of witnessing my father's savagery toward my beloved mother was so total and so all encompassing that it silenced my screams and weighted me to my chair. I froze. For what seemed like eternity I could not move a single muscle. I could only sit, and stare, and breathe in and out, while the world inside my head spun violently out of control. And then I began to shriek. A single piercing wail of horror. My father pulled my mother's hand out of the pot and rushing her outside, plunged her blistering, steaming hand into the snow.

I ran out and stood watching them, icy wind caught in my throat. My father was gently stroking my mother's hair. Her face was ghostly white and her teeth were chattering uncontrollably. Then she turned to look at me and snapped them shut like a trap. I was never the same after that day.

I obeyed my father in all things.

*****

Once there were eleven of us in my family—my father, my mother, my seven sisters, my beloved twin brother Nikolai and me. We lived in a small log cabin at the edge of a forest in Russia. We had no electricity, no TV, no phones; water had to be fetched from a well; the local village store was miles away; and we had to use the outhouse even during the freezing winter months.

I didn't know it while I was growing up but we were a strange family. We never went on holidays and we kept ourselves to ourselves. We hardly saw the other village folk. And when we did see them we were forbidden to talk to them. If ever they spoke to us we had to nod politely and move quickly away.

Growing up we had no friends. No one ever came around. I do not remember a single instance when even a doctor was called to the house. My mother said that she gave birth to all her children without even the assistance of a midwife. On one occasion when my father was not around she even had to cut the umbilical cord herself.

I have a very clear memory of when she went into labor with my youngest sister. How she was in agony for hours and how my oldest sister, Anastasia, dared to beg my father to call the doctor, and how he refused with cold anger. Only Anastasia and Sofia, my second oldest sister, were allowed in the room with Mama so the rest of us had to wait outside in abject fear.

Many horrifying hours later my father came out triumphantly holding a baby wrapped in a blanket. He showed us the baby, red from head to toe. When we were allowed to go into the room to see my mother, I was shocked by the heavy stench of blood and stale sweat. My eyes were drawn to a bundle of blood-soaked sheets pushed hurriedly into the corner of the bedroom. My mother lay on the bed ashen with pain. She was so exhausted she could barely smile at us. Her legs had been tied together roughly with rope.

'Why are your legs bound, Mama?' I asked in a frightened whisper.

'The baby came out feet first,' she murmured. Her voice was so faint I had to lean close to her lips to hear it.

Mother had had a breech birth and she was so torn and damaged internally that my father had tied her legs together to stop her moving and encourage her body to heal faster. Even as a small child I understood that he never called a doctor even though she could have died. It was agonizing to watch her in the following days, but two weeks later the ropes came off and she hobbled back to the endless chores that consumed her life.

Other than those two scary weeks I can't remember any other time I saw my mother at rest. Ever. She was always flushed and slaving away over the open fire, cooking, baking, scrubbing, washing, ironing, canning fruit and vegetables for the winter, and in spring, summer and autumn tending to our garden.

My father did not work. He was a hunter. He often disappeared into the ghostly fir tree forest behind our home and came back with elk, faun, rabbits, chinchillas, beavers, wood grouse, geese and snow partridges. The liver and brains were always reserved for him—they were his favorite—some cheap cuts were kept for the family, and the rest of the meat and fur was sold.

When my father was at home he demanded absolute silence from us. No one cried, no one talked, no one laughed. We were like little silent robots going about our tasks. Come to think of it I never saw my sisters or brother cry. The first time I saw my oldest sister, Anastasia, cry was when I was seven years old.

My mother was holding my sister's hands pressed within her own and whispering something to her and she was sobbing quietly.

'What's going on?' I whispered.

But nobody would tell me.

Chapter 2

It was midday and I was outside with my brother, sitting on a pile of wood logs watching him clean my father's boots when I heard a car pull up outside our house. For a moment neither of us moved. A car was an unheard of thing. Then I skidded off the logs in record time and we ran out front to look. Standing at the side of the house we saw the black Volga. I was instantly afraid. In my mother's stories black Volgas were always driven by bad men. Why was there a black Volga outside our house?

I thought of my sister crying in the kitchen.

Then like a miracle the clouds parted and golden rays of sun hit the metal of the car and gilded it with light. It had the effect of creating a halo. As if the car was a heavenly chariot. The front door of the chariot opened—a man's shoe emerged, and touched the dusty ground. I had never seen such a shiny shoe in all my life. Made of fine leather it had silver eyeholes and black laces. I can remember that shoe now. The shape of it, the stitching that held it together.

Another shoe appeared and a man I had never seen before unfolded himself out of the shining car. A short, hefty man with dark hair.

He was wearing a black shirt, blue jeans and a leather coat. A thick gold chain hung around his neck. As I watched, another man got out of the passenger seat. He was dressed almost identically, down to the thick gold chain. Neither looked like he had descended from heaven. Both had swarthy, closed faces. They did not say anything or call out. They just stood next to the car with an air of expectancy.

Then our front door opened and my father stood framed in it. He moved aside and Anastasia appeared beside him dressed in her best clothes.

He turned to her and said, 'Come along then.'

She turned to face him. Her lips visibly trembled.

'Neither fur, nor feather,' my father said. It was the Russian way of saying good luck.

'Go to the devil,' my sister whispered tearfully. That was the acceptable Russian way of securing good luck.

'Anastasia,' I called, and my father turned his head and glared at me.

I froze where I stood, no further sounds passing my lips. Anastasia did not look at me; her lips were pressed firmly together. I knew that look. She was trying not to cry. She picked up a small bag—I found out later my mother had packed it for her while we were all asleep—and walked with my father toward the men. One of the men opened the back door and in the blink of an eye my sister slipped through. I remembered thinking how small and defenseless she looked once inside the car.

My father and the men exchanged a few words. Then an envelope exchanged hands. The men climbed into their shiny car and drove off with my sister in it. I felt confused and frightened. My brother slipped his hand into mine. His hand was rough with mud from cleaning my father's boots. My father, my brother and I stood and watched the car as it drove on the empty dirt road in a cloud of dust. While my father was still outside I ran into the kitchen through the back door where my mother was peeling potatoes.

'Where are they taking Anastasia, Mama?' I cried.

My mother put the knife and the potato down on the table and gestured for me to come nearer. Her eyes were bright with unshed tears and her cheeks were white, waxy and transparent. Bewildered and anxious I went to her. Immediately, she grabbed me and hugged me so tightly her thin bones jagged into my flesh, and the breath was squeezed out of me. Her hands were freezing cold and the top of my shoulder where her chin was pressed in was becoming wet with her tears.

Abruptly, as if she had just remembered herself, she sniffed and put me away from her.

'Go and play with your dolls,' she said, wiping her eyes and cheeks on her sleeves.

'But where have they taken Anastasia?' I insisted. I could not understand where my sister had gone with the men.

'Your sister has a new life now,' she said, her voice hollow with despair, and picking up the knife and the half-peeled potato, resumed her task of making dinner.

'But where has she gone?' I persisted. I would never have dared insist with my father, but I knew I could with Mama.

My mother squeezed her eyes shut, the pupils twitching under their purple veined lids. 'I don't know,' she sobbed suddenly.

'What do you mean?' I asked.

My mother took a deep breath, her nostrils flaring out. With her eyes tightly shut and gripping the knife and potato so hard that her knuckles showed white she said, 'Anastasia has been sold. She will never be coming back. Best you go play with your dolls now.'

Her voice was unusually harsh, but that did not deter me. 'Sold?' I frowned. My child brain could not comprehend why my sister had to be sold. 'Why did we sell her, Mama?'

The knife clattered to the ground, the potato fell with a dull thud and rolled under the table. My mother began to rock. Violently. Like a person who has lost her mind. Her body tipping so far back on the stool I was afraid she would topple backwards. Harsh racking sobs came from her. No one would have believed that a woman that small and shriveled up could have inside her such a river of pain and anguish. It flowed out of her relentlessly, quickly and with shocking intensity.

'My daughter, my daughter,' she wailed. 'Oh, Lena, my Lena.'

I was so shocked to see the state my mother was in I didn't know what to do. I was used to seeing her cry, and I had come to accept her suffering as the way things were, but I had never seen her in this way, with her eyes unfocused and ugly sounds tearing out of her gaping mouth.

Sofia came running into the kitchen. Pushing me out of the way she grabbed my mother's hysterically swaying body and held it close to her body until the sobs were purged and she became as limp as a rag. Trembling, my mother separated from my sister.

She nodded a few times as if to indicate that she was all right and all was well again. Then she dropped to the floor and, on her hands and knees, found the knife and the potato as we stood, numb and watching. Wordlessly, she resumed peeling her potatoes. Her thin white face was tight with the effort of controlling her emotions.

My mother spent the whole day preparing elaborate dishes for our dinner that night. My sisters had set the table as if it was Christmas or Easter and we took our places silently. My sister's chair had been taken away and pushed up against the wall. I saw my mother glance at the chair and cover her mouth with her hand.

My father grabbed some schnapps glasses from the shelf and, filling them with vodka, took a glass to Mama She gazed sadly at the glass and dashed the contents down her throat. My father's eyes found hers and she swallowed hard to get the liquid down. I could hear the sound of her swallowing as clearly as I could hear my heartbeat.

Without Anastasia we began our feast. And a great feast it was. For starters we had black bread dipped in goose fat and pickled fish. Except for my father, who ate heartily, everybody else hardly touched their food. My mother's fork only clinked against her plate.

We kept our eyes on our plates. Years of being with my father had taught us that both his 'up' and 'down' moods were equally dangerous and explosive times, when anything could happen.

'By Saint Nichols, eat,' my father roared.

We all ate. Even Mama.

My father laughed and called for more vodka. The second course was beet and beef bone soup. My father drank his soup in high spirits.

The main course was roast cock with root vegetables, and the potatoes that Mama had peeled that afternoon. I looked at my father. He seemed oblivious to our frightened faces, our furtive glances at him, and the horror on my mother's sunken face.

He forked meat and vegetables into his mouth and nodded. 'I have a bad memory,' he joked merrily, 'but by God, Catherine, you remind me of why I married you at every mealtime.'

More vodka was consumed. All the while my father, his ears red, and grinning as if he had won something wonderful, sang, 'Ne uyesjai golubchick moi' (Don't go away, my little pigeon). He seemed an idiot then, but of course, that was only an illusion. My father was a bear killer. A thief of animal souls.

Stewed fruit, cheese, and more vodka were brought to the scarred wooden table. My father helped himself to fruit with shouts of extravagant joy. 'Slava Bogu!' (Glory be to God). The drunker and the louder he got, the more silent the table became.

Without warning he slammed his fist on the table. 'Why the fuck is everybody behaving as if this is a funeral?' he demanded. 'For sixteen years I fed that girl. Isn't it about time she contributed something towards the well-being of this family? We can't have any permanent drains on our family coffers.' My father squinted at us all. 'Is there anybody sitting at this table who disagrees with me?'

Nobody spoke.

His hand crashed down on the table again—plates jumped, a glass overturned. One of my sisters whimpered with fear. His blazing eyes swung around aggressively and landed on me. I realized then that everyone

else had kept their heads lowered except me. I held his eyes. For a second something flashed in them but I was too young to understand what that might be.

Then he leaned forward, his entire attention on me. At that moment there was no one else in the room except him and me. I stared into his eyes and realized that nothing lurked there. His eyes were dead and soulless.

'Am I wrong, Lena?' he asked softly, with such menace that the atmosphere in the room changed. My father had found his target.

But for some strange reason I was not afraid. He was wrong to sell my sister. He should not even have sold the bear cubs after he shot their mother. I opened my mouth to tell him that, but under the table Nikolai took my hand and clenched it so hard, I cried out instead.

'Yes, yes, you are right,' my mother intervened suddenly. Her voice was high and shaky.

My father turned away from me and looked at her. She looked small and hunched, an unworthy opponent to the bear killer, but the horrible tension was broken. A grin crossed his face suddenly and he wagged a finger jovially at her. 'You do know that your daughter is an unbroken horse, don't you?'

'She is only young. She will learn,' my mother responded quickly. Her voice was firmer than I had ever heard it.

'She'd better. Unbroken horses are worthless to their owners.'

My mother did a rare thing. She maintained eye contact with him while his mood was uncertain. Maybe because she had been weak and let Anastasia be sold, that night she found it necessary to stand her ground and protect me from my father's wrath.

After that, the night became a blur. All I really remember was the way we huddled around that table full of the kinds of food we usually only dreamed of, and yet none of us was able to eat a thing. And I recall in gory detail the way my big, strong father swept my mother off her feet and danced her around and around the samovar while she moved inside the circle of his great arms like a wooden doll.

We were all tucked up in bed that night when I awakened to the sound of someone at the front door. I hopped over my sisters' sleeping bodies and looked out of the window, and saw a sight I will never forget as long as I live. In the light of the moon my mother was naked and running away from the house. Her long dark hair was loose and streaming behind her. I could only stare at her ghostly white body in amazement. Then my father ran after her and caught her. Sobbing loudly she curled into a ball in his arms.

Gently, with great tenderness, he picked her up and carried her back into the house. I never understood the scene I had witnessed. Even now the memory makes me feel guilty as if I had seen something I shouldn't have. Something private that my mother would not have wanted me to see. I was always aware that she never wanted us to know that she loved my father to the exclusion of everything and everyone else. Even after everything he did. And even though she knew he planned to sell us all one by one.

After that strange feast, all talk of Anastasia was forbidden. The only person I could ever mention her name to was Nikolai and even then we spoke in whispers.

'Where do you think she is now?' I asked.

'I don't know. Maybe she is working for someone.'

'Doing what?'

'Accounting,' my brother said slowly. 'Rich people always need accountants.'

'But Anastasia is terrible at maths,' I countered.

My brother frowned. 'Maybe she is an English teacher like Mama was in Moscow before she met Papa.'

I nodded. That made sense. 'Yes, Mama did always say that Anastasia's English was the best. Do you think she is wearing fine clothes and living in a really grand house in Moscow?'

'Maybe.'

'Do you think she remembers us?'

'Of course.'

'Do you think she'll come back and see us?'

My brother's response was immediate and held a finality that I never forgot. 'No.'

Chapter 3

A year passed. Our family grew more silent. As was the custom in Russia, when someone left, their things were kept carefully until their return. Anastasia's chair sat against the wall like a silent reminder of our loss.

Two days after I turned eight I saw my mother folding her precious lace, the genuine point d'Alençon with the old and rare pattern. Once when she had lived in a grand house it had graced her bosom. Now it belonged to a vanished world. She placed it carefully onto a piece of tissue. Curiously, I went to her and ran my finger along the intricate pattern.

'Be careful,' my mother warned. 'It is very fragile.'

'Why are you packing your lace, Mama?' I whispered. We had all learned to keep our voices low. Other than the sound of the piano when my father was away we had all been reared in pure silence. It was so still and quiet I could hear my father turning the pages of the book he was reading.

The candlelight that illuminated my mother's face cast deep shadows under her cheekbones and brow. 'I'm giving it to Sofia. She is going away tomorrow.'

I felt clammy-cold. 'Has she been sold too?'

My mother looked at me. The seasons had wearied her. She seemed more fragile than the lace. For a moment my childish mind even entertained a fantasy that she was not a real person, only a ghost. The moment was infused with odor of candle wax. We stared at each other in the uncertain light. Her eyes were unblinking wells of pain. Something passed between us. A flickering. You cannot know it unless you have experienced it. I was only a child, but at that moment I was ancient. I understood her.

I wanted to take her into my arms and tell her I would protect her as if she were the child and I were her mother. I would save her. I would take her away from all her pain and suffering. I would kill my father while he slept. But you can't put your arms around what is already gone. Because at that moment I heard her heart. She was not asking me to kill my father, she was begging me to forgive her. Finally she opened her mouth.

'Yes, she *too* has been sold,' she said flatly.

Her tone made me see red. With all the foolishness of youth I blamed her. How I regret it now. 'Why?' I demanded under my breath.

'It is her fate. There is nothing you or I can do about it.'

'Where is she going to?' I asked in a frightened whisper.

'I don't know.' Mother's voice was listless.

Immediately I blurted out, 'Will I be sold one day too?'

There was such a long pause; I thought she might not answer me. 'Yes,' she said suddenly.

I stared at her. 'But, Mama, if we all go away who will protect you from Father?'

Her answer stunned me. 'When you are all gone, I will leave this world.' The words trembled like a candle flame in a draft. At that moment she reminded me of a precious china bowl. So fragile. It felt as if I was holding my mother in my hands—one careless move and she would shatter. And a flash of fully grown, burning hatred for my father overwhelmed me.

'I hate Papa,' I whispered vehemently.

For a moment it was as if I had not spoken or she had not heard me. There was no discernible reaction. And then her eyes flared and she grabbed my shoulders and shook me so hard my teeth rattled.

'Never let anyone else in this house hear you say that about your father again!' she whispered fiercely.

I was so shocked I could only nod.

'Good,' she said quietly, her fearful eyes darting toward the door.

'I don't *ever* want to leave you, Mama.'

Her face crumpled. 'When your turn comes you will leave.'

My immediate concern and fear was for my brother. 'Will I be parted from Nikolai?'

'Yes.'

Her answer was like stone falling into my soul. I stared at her, horrified. 'But...'

'That's enough now. Don't tell Nikolai. Don't tell anyone else. Be strong and brave, little bird. You were born under a lucky star. Somehow all will be well for you. I don't know how it will be for your brothers and sisters, but for you the sun will shine brightly.' She gathered me in her arms and kissed me on my forehead.

She tried to hide it, but I had always known that Nikolai and I were her favorites. She loved us the most. We were the golden ones, the ones that took after my father. We were the only ones with gray eyes, fair hair and long limbs.

'I love you, Mama,' I said softly.

Her eyes welled up with tears. 'I don't deserve your love,' she said. 'But I cling to it because the shreds of my sanity are hung on it. I look forward to the day I leave my cowardly deeds behind and pass away.'

That night I woke up in the middle of the night and leaving Nikolai's warm body went to Sofia. She was awake. She opened her arms and I burrowed into them. Around us my sisters slept peacefully.

'Sofia,' I asked. 'Are you afraid?'

'No, I'm not. I'll go and get help. I'll come back one day and save all of you.'

'Anastasia didn't come back.'

'But I'll come back. Somehow I'll find a way to come back.'

'I'll miss you.'

'When you have your feast tomorrow, I want you to eat. I want you to eat a lot. For me, OK? Because I'm just going for a while. I'm definitely coming back.'

'Should I tell Nikolai to eat a lot too?'

'Yes, tell him to eat a lot too.'

'I love you,' I whispered, and felt a heavy weight in my heart.

'I love you too,' she said, and held my hand. Hers was trembling uncontrollably, but she managed to give mine a weak squeeze.

*****

But Sofia did not come back. Her chair joined Anastasia's. Then Ivana's chair joined theirs. Alexandra's and Danilova's chairs followed. I was eleven years old when my two sisters, Nikolai and I sat around my mother's bed as she lay dying. Her bedroom was thick with the sick-sweet smell of deterioration. For the first time ever I heard my father ask my mother if he should call a doctor for her, but she shook her head gently and turned her face away from him. She wanted to go. She wanted to leave him. And exit the terrible world she was trapped in. He walked out of the room. I watched him walk out into the living room and simply stand there, immobile and dazed. He looked like the stags he shot.

Her descent was startlingly fast.

Who knows what disease ate her insides or for how long it had lived inside her? It looked as if she had been sucked out from inside. Her face became a solid yellow. She was only forty, but inside her body, all her organs were shutting down one by one, her liver, kidneys, the lungs, the heart. Her breathing slowed until every exhalation became a ghastly choking rattle that exited painfully from her mouth. When I held her reddened and gnarled hand, it was still warm, but she was already gone. I held that hand—the skin had never recovered from being boiled all those years ago—and twisted and re-twisted the cheap ring on her finger, until it became cold.

Father got drunk. He went out into the freezing night and falling on his knees swore at the sky. I stood at the window and saw the white trunks of the birches shining dimly through the dark. I went outside with a blanket. The air I inhaled was so cold it stabbed like a jagged piece of ice in my lungs. He looked up at me. The last time I had looked this deeply into his eyes was at the feast after Anastasia's departure.

His eyes were pained hollows in his face. So he was not totally dead inside. Strange, but perhaps he had loved her. I found no love or pity in my heart for him. Not one tiny bit. My heart was as cold as ice. I spread the blanket on his shoulders and left him there. I did that for my mother. It was what she would have done. While she was lying in her bedroom and her soul probably still not yet left, I didn't want to grieve her. But that was the last thing I would do for him.

We buried my poor sad Mama's body in a grave that my father and brother dug up at the side of the house. Nobody cried. We were all frozen. With grief and fear. Without my mother I realized that her children were in more danger than ever from my father.

Chapter 4

Two days after her funeral my father took my brother to sleep in his room. That night I awakened to a scream. I listened again and I thought I heard my brother crying. I sprang out of bed. My sister grumbled and, turning over, went back to sleep. I ran to my father's door and knocked on it.

'Go to sleep, Lena,' my father shouted.

At that time I was surprised that my father knew it was me, but now, I know it was because he knew that only I would ever dare to disobey him. It would be no one else knocking on his door at that time of the night.

'Is Nikolai all right?' I asked.

For a few ominous seconds the silence stretched. 'I'm fine, Lena. Go to sleep,' Nikolai called out, but his voice was trembling and strained.

'Are you sure?' I insisted.

'Yes. Go away,' he called out, louder and more firmly.

I stood for a few more minutes outside the door fighting with the strong and unreasonable urge to turn the handle and enter my father's bedroom. I even put my hand on the handle. But the silence inside the room frightened me. I knew I should not enter. I knew my brother did not want me to enter. I thought of my mother running naked in the snow. Somehow I knew this would be similar.

Reluctantly, I went to bed and lay awake for hours listening, but there were no further noises.

The next morning I went to the outhouse and found Nikolai's hair in the bucket. I ran out calling for him. He was in the kitchen. I touched his hair. Chunks were missing; it was roughly shorn so that in some places his skull showed. He pulled his head away from my fingers. I looked into his eyes and Nikolai was changed. He was like a stranger. He could not look me in the eye.

'What is it?' I begged.

'Nothing,' he said curtly.

'What happened last night?'

'Nothing happened,' he said sharply, and walked away from me.

I stood and stared after him. I could not understand it. Nikolai was not another person. He was a moveable extension of me. For the most part we didn't even have to speak. We knew what the other was thinking. Always. In fact, my mother said she had never heard anybody else play a duet with such perfect timing as when we played together. It was like one person with four hands.

*****

When my father came home he was absolutely furious about what my brother had done to his hair. He gave my brother a package and told him to wear it. My brother went into my father's bedroom and came out saying he would not wear it.

'Do you want Lena to wear it?' my father asked, and in his tone lurked something sinister.

My brother went white. He went back into the bedroom and came out wearing a dress! My sisters and I stared at my brother, speechless with horror.

*****

'Let's run away together,' I whispered to my brother.

'Where? Where will we go to, Lena?' he asked resentfully. 'The grand house where Anastasia is teaching mathematics?'

I was shocked at how changed he was. It was as if I was talking to my mother. All hope had vanished. Only a bitter shell remained.

'What's wrong with you?'

He looked at me sadly. 'Everything.'

*****

The winter passed, and another chair stood empty against the wall. Nikolai and I turned sixteen. All thoughts of running away had long since been extinguished. There was no need to run away. I saw it with so much more clarity—we would be sold and that would be our escape. All that was left of our family was Nikolai, my two younger sisters and me.

Next it would be my turn. But when the time came, my father skipped me and sold Zena, who was a year younger than me. I could not understand it. Then I was seventeen when the black Volga came for my youngest sister.

All that were left were Nikolai and me.

*****

Nikolai had become a man and I a woman. He was nearly as tall as my father, but neither of us could stand up to Papa It was the mahout effect. When the elephant is a baby, the mahout will tie it to an iron post. The baby will try and try and eventually learn that there is no way to get loose. When it has grown up the mahout can tie it to the flimsiest stick and the elephant will not try to extricate itself because it has been conditioned to think that no post can be beaten. My brother and I had been conditioned to obey.

That spring we turned eighteen. Summer came and went. It was autumn when Nikolai smiled with relief and squeezing my hand said, 'Don't worry. I think he is not going to sell either of us.'

*****

'Tomorrow is your turn. Be prepared to go,' my father said less than a week later. His voice was very cold and mean.

My brother stared at him in shock. That evening I caught my brother by the hand and took him to the side of the house, to mother's grave. I turned him around to face me.

'Nikolai, I'll come back for you. I don't care how I do it. I will come back. Will you wait here for me?'

'No you won't,' he said sadly and shook his head. His eyes were defeated and exhausted. 'I won't wait for you.'

'Please,' I begged.

He searched my face curiously. At that moment he reminded me of an animal. A dumb animal that was trying to figure out what you wanted it to do. I hated my father with a vengeance then.

'None of the others have. Nobody comes back,' he said with a finality that terrified me.

'But I will. On Mamas grave I promise I will. Will you promise on Mama's grave you will wait?'

'I wish he had sold me instead,' he muttered.

'Don't wish that. If he sells you I won't know where to find you. Anyway, he will never sell you.'

The intolerable situation he was in struck both of us. We never ever spoke about it. I dropped my eyes so I would not look at his shame.

'Yes, you are right. He will never sell me,' he agreed, and there was an odd inflection in his voice.

I looked up at him.

'Please. You must trust me that I will come back for you.'

He rubbed his earlobes and nodded, but did not meet my eyes.

I grabbed his hand. 'Look at me and promise, Nikolai,' I demanded fiercely.

'I promise,' he said. 'I promise on Mother's grave I will wait until you come.'

I smiled. I had his word. I was at peace. He smiled back. I touched his cheek.

'Oh, Nikolai. I don't know what it will be like without you.'

His Adam's apple bobbed. 'You will be fine, Lena.' Tears ran down our faces.

When the men came the next day we stood facing each other. 'Mind how you go, beautiful sister of mine.'

'Until we meet again, my darling,' I said kissing him hard on his lips. Outside the Volga idled quietly.

'Remember your promise,' I reminded, my fingers curling around his. They were rough with work. He tried to pull his hand away but I wouldn't let go. I stared into his eyes.

He nodded distantly.

'You must wait for me.'

'I will.'

'Neither fur nor feather,' he said. His voice was listless.

'Go to the devil,' I said softly.

And I went out into the cold morning toward the black Volga. The Volga never aged. The men were different...and the same.

They passed my father a thick envelope. He did not open it. He simply called my name. 'Lena.'

'Yes, Father?'

'It's time to go. Obey these men as you would me.'

I did not look at him or answer him.

Chapter 5

The men did not look at or speak to me after I got into the car or as we drove away from my home. I clasped my hands tightly and remained silent. Ten minutes into the journey and the man in the passenger seat turned to look at me. He had slightly slanted Asian eyes and olive skin. His eyes were so black and cold they made me tingle.

'We don't want to hurt you. If you behave there will be no need for us to hurt you. Are you going to behave?'

I nodded. Of course I was going to behave. What else was I going to do? I was in a black Volga with two of the most dangerous-looking men I had ever seen being driven to God knows where. The driver looked into the rear-view mirror me at me. He had dark hair and cruel blue eyes. There was something low and mean about him.

They took me to a hotel where there was electricity, running water, a toilet that flushed, and the rustle of Russian newspapers. I slept on a comfortable bed and awakened to a breakfast of strawberry jam on French bread. They did not introduce themselves, but I learned from their conversation that the men were called Timur and Borka. Timur was obviously the leader and Borka was the mean idiot driving the car.

It was after we stopped for a bathroom break that I realized that they had forgotten to lock the doors. I did nothing. Just sat quietly at the back. Waiting. In the middle of a village near a crowded tavern where it looked like there was a celebration of some kind as men were standing around talking and drinking, I opened the door while the car was still moving, and rolled out.

The jarring pain of the tarmac was incredible. The car sped on as I lay on the road, winded and in terrible pain. But not for long. It screeched to a halt a few yards away. I wanted to run, but I could barely move. The car began reversing so fast it looked like a blur to my panicked eyes. With a burst of energy and a vicious twist of pain that made me scream I forced myself to my hands and feet and, rising upright, began to run.

I ran as fast as my wounded body would allow me to. I ran toward the celebrating villagers. There were men there. They were many and my captors were only two. They could help me, surely they would. I called out to them, and their faces turned in my direction, and they stared at me, running, hopping, limping. Defenseless.

Then calmly, as if with one mind, all of them turned away from the troublesome sight of a woman being chased by a black Volga and looked down into their drinks. They did not want to get involved. It was none of their business.

The force of Borka landing on me knocked me off my feet and we crashed onto the grass verge. For a while I was too winded to speak. Then he hauled me up roughly by the hair, and slapped me so hard my head snapped back.

From the side of the road Timur screamed, 'Don't mark her, you fucking animal.'

I could taste the blood from my split lip, but I looked up at Borka defiantly.

Something flared in his eyes. Rabid lust. I had never seen anyone look at me like that before and it shocked me. The greed was replaced by ugly anger. 'Stupid fucking bitch,' he shouted and pulled me toward the car.

The other man peered at my face and turned angrily toward Borka. 'You fucking idiot,' he screamed. 'You cut her.'

Borka immediately looked defensive. 'It's nothing. It will heal.'

'If you touch her again I'll break your fucking legs. And take that fucking look out of your eyes and stuff it up your shitty ass. Nobody is fucking spitting in my rice bowl.'

'I didn't do nothing,' Borka muttered with a surly curl of his lips.

'Damn right. And you won't either.'

'What's the big deal anyway? I was only going to fuck her mouth or her ass. Who's gonna know?'

The look Timur leveled at Borka was fierce and poisonous. 'If you want to fuck something, pick up a dirty whore tomorrow night.'

Borka clenched his jaw in mute anger.

Timur turned toward me. I was frightened of him. He had the eyes of a man who knows no limits. They glittered dangerously the way a sharp knife does. 'Get in the car. Now,' he snarled.

I obeyed immediately. I was sore all over as I stumbled to the car. When we were in and the doors were locked, Timur twisted around to face me. 'I give you freedom and what do you do?'

'I'm sorry,' I said through my swelling lip.

'Do you want to be tied up and gagged from now on?'

I shook my head slowly.

'Another stunt like that and you *will* be tied up and gagged and put in the boot of the car. Are we clear?'

I nodded.

He took a handkerchief out of his pocket and handed it to me. 'Wipe your mouth.'

I took the handkerchief and wiped my mouth. He immediately grasped my chin with his fingers. His skin was extraordinarily soft. He turned my face to either side to assess the damage. Expressionlessly he released my chin. In the rear-view mirror Borka was watching me.

'Show me your hands,' he ordered.

I held my hands out. They were scraped and bleeding. He twisted my wrists and saw that my hands were scraped right down to my elbows.

Cursing, he reached down and pulled my skirt right up to my panties. I was so ashamed—no one had seen my thighs for as long as I could remember, and I wanted to cover them with my hands, but I didn't. I knew he would be furious. One of my knees was bleeding and there were scratches and cuts on my shins. Timur cursed again and turned around. I pulled my dress back over my knees.

After that no more was said. Borka drove silently until we arrived at a farmhouse in the middle of nowhere. There were chickens in coops at the side of the house and a barn a few yards away. I could see a well, too.

'Get out,' Timur barked.

I got out and walked with them toward the house. The air was cold and I had a sick, horrible feeling in my stomach.

A woman opened the door to us. She was wearing a headscarf and a dirty apron. She looked like a farmer. She must have been about forty years old. She had big, muscular arms and grit-filled nails. Her face was broad, her complexion florid, and her eyes were the color of dirty dishwater. For a flash of a second they registered surprise and something else—something I had only ever encountered in men's eyes. Then she concealed it and focused on my lip.

'What the hell happened?' she asked. Her accent was thick and unrefined.

'Ask Borka,' Timur snapped rudely, and brushing past her went into the darkened interior of the house.

She did not look at Borka who was standing behind me. Instead she turned her ruddy face toward me and smiled. It was an unpleasant smile. 'Your sisters never gave so much trouble.'

'My sisters?' I gasped. In my chest my heart leapt at the possibility, no matter how remote, that I would see my lost family again. Hope swirled in my head making me feel almost dizzy.

She narrowed her eyes and folded her thick, manly arms around her midriff. 'Yes, all your sisters passed through here.'

'Where are they now?'

For a few seconds she did not answer me, simply looked at me speculatively. Finally, she moved aside and said, 'Come in. We'll talk inside.'

Immediately, eagerly, I stepped into her house. Inside it was gloomy and stank of grease and cooking and a heady mixture of herbs. As my eyes adjusted to the gloom I saw that I was in an ordinary Russian farmhouse, one where life revolved around the stove. As my eyes swung around the poor furniture they fell upon a large metal cage with straw at the bottom of it.

Just as suddenly as I had seen it I was shoved roughly to the ground. Before I could react, I was pulled hard and pushed into the cage. It was only about four feet long by about five feet high so I could neither stand nor lie in it. I crouched against the bars while she padlocked the door. I did not scream or shout. I knew it was no use.

As my eyes got even more used to the gloom I saw that everything was covered in a thick layer of soot and grease. Blackened pots and a long-handled pan sat on the stove. Even the bars of the cage were dirty and sticky. The strong smell of herbs was coming from the many different varieties that she was drying on newspapers spread on every available surface. I could make out rosemary, oregano, and sage.

Timur sat at the rough wooden table eating bread and cheese. He ate quickly, his eyes resting on the woman.

'You'll have to clean up her wounds,' he told her.

'Don't worry. They are superficial. They'll heal on their own. I will keep her until she's broken in.'

'You know the rules,' he said. There was warning in his eyes.

'Yeah, she better be as good as new,' Borka added threateningly, cutting himself a slice of cheese and stuffing it into a hunk of bread.

After they had eaten they left and the woman ignored my attempts to talk to her or ask her about my sisters.

When night fell, she lit the lamps and opened the door to what must have been her larder. A waft of cold air pungent with the smell of herbs drifted into the house. I could see shelves stocked with jars upon jars of elixirs, honeycombs, pickled vegetables, garlic, and fruit. She came out again with some vegetables. She cut the vegetables, took out a piece of meat from her refrigerator and made a stew. The smell of gristle frying made my mouth water. I had not eaten for a whole day. She passed a steaming bowl to me through a small door in the cage.

I was starving so I ate it quickly. She must have drugged my food for I started to feel so sleepy I could not keep my eyes open.

And then I remembered no more.

Chapter 6

I woke up groggy and still inside the cage, but I was naked. Some foul-smelling green medicine had been applied to my cuts and wounds. When I saw her watching me I instinctively tried to hide myself with my hands.

'Do you think you have anything I haven't seen before?' she taunted and laughed so hard her whole body shook.

I could not rise from my hands and knees position so I curled up into a ball and watched her go about her business. I knew she would not hurt me, at least, not physically. The men had seemed determined to keep me in as good a condition as they could. I was worth a lot of money to them. When I said I needed to go to the toilet she heaved herself off the table where she had been peeling onions, grabbed a bowl and was about to thrust it into the cage.

'I can't go in a bowl,' I protested, shocked.

'Then you will soil yourself.' Her voice was hard. She pushed the bowl through the little door my food had come in through.

So I went in the bowl. It was the most humiliating thing that had happened to me. She stood over me with her arms folded and watched while I squatted over the bowl and pissed slowly in spurts. It was very difficult to do without wetting myself, or the straw that I would have to sleep on. Some urine splashed on my legs.

'Can I have some toilet paper to clean myself with, please?' I pleaded.

'Toilet paper is only for when you shit,' she said rudely, and carried the bowl out of the house.

I watched her greedily eat an open sandwich of sliced sausages on rye bread. Afterwards, she tied her scarf tightly around her head, put on her coat and galoshes, and went out. A gust of freezing wind hit me in the chest before she closed the door. I heard her footsteps die away. A dog barked. Even though the stove was on I was so cold my fingers and toes were icy. I covered myself with some of the straw and waited for her to come back.

It was midday when her footsteps returned. She opened the door and came in. Her hands were red. She set a bucket of water on the floor. The galoshes gleamed in the dim interior of her house. She ladled a mug full of water from the pail, rinsed her mouth out and spat the water into the slop bucket. She ladled another mug of water and slowly poured it through the top of the cage. I caught it in my mouth. Like an animal.

With a grunt she left me. Again she ate—two helpings of casserole and bread—without offering me any. After her meal she went back out, taking with her a bucket, and returned only when it was nearly dark.

There was a layer of soot and grime on my skin. I felt as if the smell had seeped into me. 'Can I have some water to wash myself, please?'

'I didn't bring it to waste on you,' she sneered.

Not only was I not allowed to wash, I was forced to defecate in a bowl and clean myself with a bit of newspaper while she stood watching. I knew what she was trying to do. She was trying to humiliate me. She was trying to make me believe that I was no better than an animal. She was trying to break me. And maybe she did.

When it was dark she lit the lamps and began to cook. She made an omelet in the long-handled pan. After she had eaten she poured some of the leftover casserole into a bowl and brought it to me.

I stared at it in shock. Disgusting woman. It was the same bowl I had pissed in and shat in. I pushed it out of the cage, away from me. I was hungry, but I refused to eat it. She took it away wordlessly and poured it into the slop pail where I had seen her throw away last night's vegetable peels.

'Next meal you eat you will have to beg for,' she said, and pushing the cage closer to the stove, switched off the lights and shuffled to her bedroom. When she closed the door the place was in darkness except for the red glow from the stove. I was shivering and frightened—not of her, but of the future. It stretched dark and terrible. I bit my fist and stared at the cracks in the cement floor.

I waited until I heard her snoring and then I clapped my hand tightly over my mouth and let the sobs that were deep inside me flow out. They came like a river until my tongue felt stiff, my throat was painful, and my eyes were burning. But there was relief.

When the sobs stopped I hugged myself tightly and thought of the comforting feel of Nikolai's fair head close to mine. I remembered the clean smell of his hair, his sweet breath. The familiar soothing feel of his skin against mine. How I missed him. I wondered what he would be doing. He would be in bed by now. In Father's bed.

My resolve hardened and I knew then that I would survive. I would survive this cage and anything else they threw at me. I swore to myself that I would do whatever was necessary to get back. To rescue him from my father's clutches.

Slowly I comforted myself.

And eventually, the fire crackling in the stove, the humming of the refrigerator, and the ticking clock put me to sleep. I dreamed of that New Year. My mother was still alive. My father had gone to ghostly fir tree forest to hunt for game, and my brother and I were in the woods to collect kindling, but instead we had built a snowman. It was so huge I had to climb on my brother's shoulders to place the snowman's head on top of his body. Our hands were freezing, our noses were red, and our ears stinging, but we had stood back and looked in awe at what we had done. I was happy in my dream.

For two days I hung on, and refused to eat, but hunger coupled with the sight of a pig's ears boiling under a cloud of steam is a cruel master. I did not turn to watch her raise the pig's ear in a slotted spoon, and settle it on a plate, but some part of me saw it. I did not stare while she sat at the table and sliced into it with her knife only a few feet away from me, but my mouth ran with saliva all the same. The smell of horseradish cucumber relish and sour pickles made my chest heave with hunger. I heard her gulp her beer noisily and knew as she did that I was not going to win this war. It was not worth winning. I caved in.

'Please can I have some food?'

She turned to me. 'Did you say something? My hearing is not good.'

'Please, can I have some food?'

She nodded and put the pig's ear into the bowl and pushed it through the little hole in the cage. No spoon, no cutlery. Just cramming the pig's ear into my mouth with my filthy fingers. She looked at me and laughed. I didn't care anymore. So she had reduced me to the status of a naked wild animal. And so fucking what? I must survive and find a way to rescue my brother.

I could see the scabs on my knees beginning to heal. I picked at them. That made her angry. 'Do you prefer to stay longer in the cage?'

I stopped picking at them.

Two days, maybe three passed. She came and stood by the cage.

'Push your nipples through the cage bars,' she ordered.

'I won't,' I said. And I meant it. I hated her and what she had done to me. What I had become.

'Then you will stay in that cage until you learn to obey me.'

I stood no chance while I was in the cage. I had to get out of the cage. I pushed my breasts through the bars.

'Good,' she praised, and put her mouth on one of my nipples and sucked it.

I was so shocked I reared back. For some seconds we stared at each other. Then slowly I put my breasts back between the cold steel bars. I closed my eyes and endured while she sucked them until they felt quite raw.

She wanted to humiliate me to show me that all the things I thought were disgusting and beneath me could be done to me, against my will and with impunity. And there was not a damn thing I could do to stop it. She laughed softly and deliberately grabbed my breasts in her rough hands and squeezed them painfully.

'What would you do for a nice hot towel?' she sneered.

I didn't answer her, but I felt so soiled and dirty, the thought of a hot towel was like a flash of something delicious from the past.

That night I was fed properly: a large piece of roasted reindeer meat. It's true, I fell on it and ate it like an animal.

'When can I get out of the cage?' I asked.

'Soon. Show me good behavior.'

I became a cowering submissive creature. When she asked me to, I pressed my breasts through the bars and endured her noisy cruel mouth. This time she gave me meat jelly. I knew what she was doing but what could I do? In a cage, naked, hungry, unwashed... With no opportunity for escape.

The next morning she pushed a hot towel fragrant with the smell of soap through the bars and watched while I wiped myself. It was the most delicious feeling. The sun filtered in through the grimy glass of her windows. I handed her back the towel. She rinsed it, squeezed the water and handed it back to me.

Then she passed me a bowl of warm water for my hair. I washed it as best I could. My scalp felt light again. When the fire from the stove had dried my hair she came and stood next to my cage.

'You have very beautiful hair. You'll fetch the boys a fine price.'

My temples began to throb. I couldn't think straight. 'Who will they sell me to?'

'A very, very rich man no doubt. You should consider yourself lucky. If you were not so beautiful, you would have been sold to a brothel.'

I licked my lips. 'This house stinks of cooking smells. If you slice an onion and put it into a bowl of water, it will remove the smell.'

Saying nothing she put the teakettle on the stove, but that night while making dinner she put a slice of onion into a bowl of water and left it on the kitchen table. We ate silently. She must have drugged me again, because soon I fell into a deep sleep.

When I woke up I was still naked, but I was lying on the floor. An iron leg shackle was on my right leg. A three foot chain to keep me shackled to the main post of the house.

'The key is hidden somewhere safe outside this house. So if anything happens to me you'll starve to death in here.'

'I pray nothing happens to you then,' I replied.

'Here,' she said and gave me a tomato. I bit into it. The smell and the taste of the juice on my tongue were incredible.

She watched me. 'I grew it myself. I had a good harvest this year.'

I pushed the last bit into my mouth and wiped my lips with the back of my hand.

'Would you like another?'

I nodded. Even then I knew there would be a price to pay. It was not the price of the tomato, it was the price of being out of the cage.

Chapter 7

She took off her scarf. Under it her salt and pepper hair was braided and wrapped in a crown on top of her head. Then she unbuttoned her dress and took off a grayish-white bra. Her breasts hung down, fat and pale and adorned with green veins. She asked me to suck them. I took my eyes away from them and toward her eyes. They were eager and excited. The tomato churned in my stomach. I experienced a flash of hatred for this woman. The urge to scratch her face was unbelievable. At that moment I might even have hated her more than I did my father.

And yet some part of me that did not hate her was sobbing silently. I swallowed the lump in my throat. So many thoughts ran through my head. What was to become of me? Was this how my life was going to be? I had promised Nikolai that I would come back for him. She would not win. She could bully me...for now. But in the end she would not win. I would. I would beat them all. No matter what they tried to do to my body and my mind, my spirit would rise above them and remain pure.

Nobody could sully me unless I let them.

Let her think I was doing it for her rotten tomato, or because I didn't want to go back into the cage. The truth was I was doing it because I wanted to wash with some of the water that was boiling in the pot. I could hear the lid rattling. I wanted the smell of soap. I wanted to feel clean again so I could think. So I would be prepared for what lay after her. For she was only the beginning. There would be others who would want different parts of their bodies sucked. I would not fail Nikolai.

I reached out a hand and stroked her hair. She closed her eyes and moaned. I sucked her sweaty, greasy nipples while she groaned and lamented the fact that I had to be delivered a virgin. She took off her thick woolen tights, and I did other things to her too. Things one does to survive. Things that made me sick to my stomach. Despicable things. Things that crushed my heart.

'You have a willing and delicious mouth,' she said, as she pulled on her clothes. 'You'll make someone very happy one day.'

'Can I have that tomato now?'

Even though the juice ran down my chin, the tomato did not seem sweet and juicy as the first one had. It was not the tomato. It was me. My mouth had become sour with the taste of her. While she was not looking I scrubbed my tongue with my palms.

That night she gave me homemade vodka that burned my throat. I drank it willingly. I knew what lay ahead. But I would survive. I would survive them all. God only knew how many little glasses I upended down my throat. The room blurred, and yet I froze when she turned to me, embraced me and pulled me toward her.

'You're so golden,' she said. 'I've never seen hair like yours.'

My pain became alive. It tangled with hers. She taught me to use my fingers and my mouth. I did what she asked. She stroked my hair gently and crooned encouragingly while I did it. Then she twitched and convulsed and pulled my hair when she climaxed. The sounds that tore past her open mouth were animal-like. She reminded me of a suffering animal. I stared at her bleakly; I felt dead inside. My mind had become so detached I couldn't think anymore. I fell away from her sticky skin back to the cold floor and I vomited. She cradled my head in her lap and I hated the smell of her skirt.

The days passed, the clock ticked, the refrigerator hummed, and the fire roared. A wind had started up. It rattled the window.

'Do you still have my mother's lace?'

She didn't pretend not to understand. I had guessed right. She had stolen it from my sister. She narrowed her eyes.

'Do you want it?' she asked.

'Yes, it is the last thing I have of my mother.'

'What will you do for it?'

I felt cold and numb. My mouth had twisted open like the lid of a jar and words had dropped out. 'Whatever you want.'

'How will you keep it, though? The men will take it off you.'

'I will sew it into the petticoat of my dress.'

The floor creaked underneath her weight as she slowly went into her bedroom. The lace was still wrapped in the same tissue my mother had wrapped it in. A lump came in my throat. I wanted to scream at her not to touch the tissue, not to unwrap it, not to soil it, not to change its perfume. It was my mother's. It was the only thing left of her. She put it on the floor next to me and ran her hands down my hips and between my legs. I did nothing. I was in pieces. The pieces were all mute. I didn't think I could ever be fused together again.

*****

That afternoon she had gone out and I had heard screaming and been frightened. When she came back into the house she was sweating and covered in blood.

'Slaughtered a pig,' she explained. Then she went to wash.

'Would you like to sit at the table and eat with me tonight?' she offered when she came back.

'The chain does not reach the table,' I said looking at her innocently.

She nodded and started cooking. It was getting dark outside when she unlocked my shackles.

'There are clothes laid out on the bed for you. Wear them.'

I went into her bedroom. There was a wooden bed, a cupboard and an old dresser. Her bedroom was cold. I closed the door behind me. There was only a small window and it was locked. I put on the clothes. They smelt musty and they were too big for me, but I was grateful for them. The feel of clothes after you have been naked for so long cannot be explained, only experienced. It was as if she had given me back my dignity. I was once again a human being.

Feeling strangely protected I went out to her. I had a plan. Tonight I would escape. I would get her drunk and snoring and then I would slip out.

There were lit candles on the table. It looked like the kind of thing a wife might do for her husband on their anniversary. It angered me. I stood by the door and she looked up, bunched her hands into fists, and let out a trembling sigh.

'Come to eat,' she said gruffly.

I walked to the table laden with food.

Roast pork with potatoes, buckwheat, sauerkraut, and pickled tomatoes. She had brought out her fine china: the plates had entwined roses on the edges. For the first time since I had been here I held a knife and fork in my hand. She looked at me as I cut into the pork. The delicious smell of meat wafted out. I passed it between my lips.

She sipped at her glass of wine and reached for some bread. It was a strange meal. Outside it had begun to snow. White flakes dropped from a black sky. Inside it was warm. The woman in front of me was quiet and wrapped in a blanket of some inner sorrow.

'It's snowing,' I said.

She turned her head and looked out of the window. 'Yes, soon the roads will be impassable.'

Was that some kind of warning? I licked my lips. 'How will you get provisions in?'

'I've got everything I need to see me through the winter.'

'How come you live here alone?'

She stuck a piece of meat into her mouth. I watched her mouth close around it. Outside the snow fell steadily. I stole another look at the window. When I looked back at her she was watching me.

'There is nothing for miles and miles, and lots of wild animals out there. Wild boars wolves, lynxes, brown bears. They will even come right up to the house.' She slapped her lips around a mouthful of sauerkraut. 'Aye, it will be very cold tonight. A person could freeze to death and no one would know until the snow melted again in spring, that is, if the animals don't find their corpse first.'

I cut a small piece of potato. 'Yes, it would be foolhardy to go out walking in this weather.'

'Do you like this wine?' she asked softly.

I took a sip. 'Yes, it is good.'

She smiled. 'I prefer beer or vodka myself.'

'So why did you serve wine?'

'I thought you might like it. You look the type.'

I stared at her in surprise. She was courting me. 'Thank you, for thinking of me.'

'So don't waste it. There is no one else here to drink it.'

I drank it slowly. I had a plan and it did not involve getting drunk and passing out. But as the meal wore on I began to feel more and more sleepy. Eventually, I looked at her. 'You've drugged me, haven't you?'

'Of course. I couldn't take the chance you would go wandering off on your own. Tomorrow the men will come for you and it will be more than my life's worth if they do not find you here.'

She came around my side in time to catch my falling body.

*****

I woke up chained and in my own clothes. She had dressed me while I was unconscious. I thought of her hands on my body while I lay inert. She had her back to me. She was making breakfast.

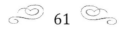

'Good morning,' I said. My mouth felt sour.

She did not answer, did not even turn to look at me. I wondered what she was up to, and suddenly remembered that last night she had said that the men were coming back to take me. No wonder I was dressed in the clothes I had come in. A small ball of fear landed in my stomach. I hated the vile things I had to do to her, but I had become used to this life, I knew what every single day brought. There was security and continuity without disturbance.

What lay in the future was suddenly frightening; it loomed filled with major shifts, new and unfamiliar situations and characters. And danger. There was even the possibility that I would not survive. Outside the world was white. The smell of food muddled my brain.

I took the toothbrush she had put beside me, which already had a tiny blob of toothpaste on it, and brushed my teeth. I spat into a bowl and turned my face in her direction.

'What time are the men coming?'

She whirled around, her face a mask of rage. 'Why are you eager for them to come and take you?'

'No,' I said, startled by her fury. 'I'm afraid of what awaits me.'

Her face softened. 'My joy, my sun, it breaks my heart to let you go. If I had the money I would buy you and keep you for myself.'

And suddenly I knew I was not so afraid of the future. Whatever was out there must be better than being caged and forced to be a sexual slave to this woman.

I didn't let my thoughts show. 'They will bring other girls for you.'

Her large chest heaved. 'No one will replace you. I will love you forever.'

My lips parted. Her declaration of love was so odd, so unexpected, so without base, and so unrequited.

'Yes, I will miss you too,' I lied.

She brought the corner of her apron to her eyes. I looked at the front door and prayed that the men would come soon.

She put before me a bowl of semolina porridge cooked in milk and sugar and a jar of jam. I looked up at her with surprise. Breakfast was always strong rye bread with sliced sausages on top.

I took a spoonful of jam—there were large pieces of berries in it—and put it on the porridge.

'Did you make the jam yourself?'

She nodded and bit into her open-top jam sandwich.

'My mother used to make jam. She would pour the foam skimmed from the boiling pot into our hands. It used to make my teeth twinge.'

She smiled showing raspberry seeds wedged between her teeth. 'There are always worms in the foam.'

At that moment I felt something akin to hatred for her. I swallowed a spoonful of semolina. My heart was pounding with my hatred.

She sat cross-legged on the floor opposite me and watched me eat my food. I did not speak and neither did she. We both knew we would never see each other again.

Chapter 8

The men came an hour later. When she heard their car, I saw her hunch as if in pain. For a while she sat very still. Then she stood up slowly, and went to the door. Borka stood at the entrance but Timur brushed past her and entered the house. He looked at me and nodded as if satisfied. Then he turned away and took a wad of money from his pocket—not half as thick as the one he had given my father—and held it out to her. She took it from him and held it in her fist.

'What's the matter with you?' he asked.

'Nothing,' she said tetchily.

'She's in love,' Borka taunted gleefully.

Zara turned and glared at him.

Timur grasped her hand roughly. 'You haven't tampered with her, have you?' he asked menacingly.

'Of course not,' flashed Zara. 'I know the rules.'

'Fucking better not have. She has to pass the medical exam.'

'If she doesn't pass it, it won't be down to me,' she said sourly.

'Seagull's word has been good so far.'

'Then you have nothing to worry about.'

Zara unlocked my iron shackle. I rubbed my ankle slowly.

'We'd better get going.'

When we were seated in the car I turned back to look at Zara standing in the doorway of her farmhouse. She did not wave, and I watched her get smaller and smaller. I would never forget her, or the humiliation she had put me through.

'How come she gets to have her ugly cunt sucked and I don't get anything?' Borka asked. He sounded like a child, petulant and whiny.

'There's more chance of you getting me to suck your stinking dick than there is of it getting in her mouth. Now can you shut the fuck up and drive? I want to get to Helga's before dark.'

Timur switched on the radio and I turned my face toward the window and watched the white landscape zoom by.

Hours later we arrived at another farmhouse. It was much bigger than Zara's. There were trucks and cars outside and lights in the windows. Another peasant woman opened the door to us and led me to a room. The windows were barred. There was a bed with a dirty sheet pulled across it. I sat on it and waited. It wasn't long before a man came. He had greasy hair.

'I am a doctor,' he announced.

He was not what I imagined a doctor to look like. Nevertheless he carried a little black bag with him.

'Take off your underwear and lie on the bed.'

I did as I was told. I bent my knees and opened my legs when he told me to and I closed my eyes at the feel of his cold instruments.

'Good,' he pronounced. 'You may dress again.'

I pulled my underwear on without meeting his eyes.

He brought an instrument that looked like a gun toward me. 'Lift your left arm.' When I lifted my left arm he held the instrument toward my skin and pressed the lever. Something shot into my arm.

'What's that?'

'It's a contraceptive that's good for two years and it's also a chip.'

'A chip?'

'If you run they will always be able to locate your exact position.'

'I won't run,' I said. My voice was dull with despair.

'Yeah,' he said tiredly.

I ran my finger along the almost unnoticeable bump under my skin.

'Don't worry, it will be all right.'

I didn't look at him. I didn't say anything. What did he expect? That I would forgive him? That I would think he was a nice guy doing an awful job? No, I didn't absolve him. Give me Timur any day. At least he didn't pretend. At least with him it was like meeting a tiger in a jungle. Your bad luck. He is hungry; you're meat. I set my eyes strongly once on his weak, greedy face and then I looked to the dirty concrete floor.

His hand came out and squeezed my shoulder. 'Well, I'll be off then,' he said uncomfortably, and he was gone.

Afterwards I was taken to a bare room with a camera. I was told to wear a black bikini and a pair of red high heels. A girl about my age came and put cosmetics on me and did my hair. She took it out of its plaits, wet it and blow-dried it into large waves that she artfully arranged around my shoulders.

'Your hair is beautiful,' she said.

I already knew that. Zara used to run her fingers through it. 'Gold,' she used to whisper. 'Gold.'

'Do you want to see yourself?' she asked.

I nodded dumbly. She held out a small oval mirror.

I looked different.

'Why am I wearing make-up?' I asked her.

'Because you are going to be photographed.'

'Why do they need my photo?'

She looked at me strangely, curiously. 'For the auction.'

'Auction? What auction?'

She glanced at the door. 'The photo will be sent to very rich men all over the world, and they will use it to decide whether they want to bid on you,' she said in a lowered voice.

I was told to stand on an X marked on the floor. I stood where I was told to and stared at the camera. The camera flashed about twenty times and then I was led back to the room with the dirty sheet.

*****

The next day we were back in the car. The Volga sped through country lanes. On either side were snowy fields and spare dwellings. There was no further conversation between the men, although Borka occasionally looked in the rear-view mirror at me. The dullness was unremitting. I slept and awoke to the same scenery.

Until the road signs indicated that we had reached Moscow.

Timur turned to me. 'You have a twin brother?' he asked emotionlessly.

'Yes,' I said, nodding eagerly. Hoping for any scraps of information or news.

'You love him?'

My nod was a lot more measured and slower. I knew what was coming.

'You try to run or do anything, and when I say anything, I mean actually anything at all that causes your owner to raise a complaint, and...' He slid his index finger across his throat. 'You will never see your brother alive again.' He paused to let his words and menacing gesture sink in. 'Do you understand?'

I looked into his cold, cold eyes and I knew that he was not lying. Fear pierced my heart like a shard of glass. He really would get into his car and drive all the way to my village and slice my brother's throat just to keep his word. I nodded vigorously. He moved close to my ear. 'And just for fun I'll let Borka rape him first.'

I swallowed hard. 'You won't have any trouble from me,' I promised.

He carried on staring at me.

'*Ever.*'

'Good. Now get into the boot.'

The rest of the journey I remember the way you remember a dream. Haphazard. Smells, sounds, a glimpse of something foreign. Half the time my head was covered, but always I could feel my mother's lace against my skin and it comforted me.

I heard them mention Germany and Holland, but I never saw anything. Always I was inside covered vehicles. Inside car boots, inside covered lorries. I knew I was crossing borders. Sometimes I was drugged. I went in and out of consciousness. We might have crossed the sea, I don't know, but I remember being very sick, vomiting. Someone cursing at me. A woman helping me clean up. Another girl with large, frightened eyes looking at me.

She had long dark hair. Maybe I was always drugged.

I think I even flew once. And then finally I woke up in the back seat of a car. Timur and Borka were long gone. The man driving had narrow shoulders and brown hair. It was dark outside, but I could see that the scenery was very different. I knew I was in a different country.

'Where are we?' I asked.

The man met my eyes in the rear-view mirror. 'It's a surprise,' he said.

Chapter 9

He had answered me in English! I was in an English speaking country. Only my mother had ever spoken to us in English. And only when my father was not around. It was already dark, with a full moon low in the sky.

'What's the time, please?' I asked.

'Six p.m.'

We traveled in silence for about another hour before the car arrived at a set of huge ornate black iron gates. I had never seen anything so magnificent. They must have stood ten feet tall. The driver got out of the car and pushed the gates open. He drove through them and we traveled on a long dark road through what seemed like fields and woodland. Though there were lampposts on either side of the road, none of them were lit. The road, too, was full of potholes and made for a bumpy ride. We passed through a half-ruined stone arch gate. Moss clung to it like a straggly beard. Suddenly the front of the castle came into view.

It was the kind of castle that could have been the inspiration for the darkest fairy tales my mother had read to me. It lay like an old man of the hill, moonlight shining on its craggy, gray face. The once proud turrets were crumbling and the ancient walls were almost totally overgrown with creepers, the windows dark and gaping. The heavy grandeur, the massiveness of the structure and its general air of disrepair made it appear gloomy and forbidding.

Surrounding it were tall, ancient trees that seemed to guard the ragged outline like an army defending its citadels. The dark green coverage enhanced the castle's sense of eeriness. Even the stones seemed to echo with terrible sadness. It looked...haunted. I felt a shiver run up my spine.

Finally we arrived at the entrance. Creepers curled around the top of it.

The driver opened his door and, locking me inside, walked up the stone steps to the great door, made of ancient oak, studded with metal and built with heavy black scrolled hinges. He lifted the rusty doorknocker and rapped it hard. For a while there was no response but just as he was about to lift the doorknocker again, there was the sound of someone unlatching the door from the inside. One half of the door creaked and groaned like a banshee as it swung open.

A slim woman stood holding a storm lantern.

I could not hear what was being said, but the driver came back to the car, opened the door, and told me to get out. I came out, feeling crumpled and stiff, and followed him to the great door. The woman was young. I guessed her to be about my age. She was very pretty with thick auburn hair and very pale skin. In the light of the lamp I could not make out the color of her eyes, but they looked like they might be pale blue. Strangely, an expression of sadness or pity crossed her eyes when she met mine, then the look was swept away and she smiled softly and said, 'Hello, Lena. I'm Misty Moran.'

'Right, my job here is done. I'm off,' said the driver.

Misty and I watched him get into his car and drive away. Then she turned to me and said, 'You'd better come in then.'

We went into the house and while she swung the heavy door closed I looked around the gray stone walls and lofty ceilings in shock. It was so unbelievably vast. I tried to imagine how many of my homes would have fit into it. One hundred? Two?

'We've had two days of storm and high winds and suffered a power cut. The electricity will be back on tomorrow.'

From the dim recesses a huge black shape moved and let out a low blood-curdling growl. My eyes widened with fear.

'That's just Ceba,' Misty dismissed. 'He's a Tibetan Mastiff. He is very fierce and can be aggressive, but if you keep out of his way he won't do anything to you.' The dog moved its massive bulk into the circle of light. His head was as big as a bear's. He looked at me with unfriendly, aloof yellow eyes.

'Down, Ceba,' ordered Misty in a stern voice, and he slunk away back to his shadowy corner. She turned to me. 'Come on then, I'll show you to your room.'

A single candle guttered at the base of the stairwell, illuminating a Roman marble statue, and the echo of our footsteps bounced off the walls and reverberated around us. We went up a curving staircase. It was dark and I could not make out much except the sensation of great space, thick walls, high ceilings, and dark wood. There were tall paintings of stern people in ancient costumes looking down on us.

'That way is the west wing. You are allowed to wander around on your own and go anywhere that is not locked, except for the Lady Anne tower in the west wing.'

I nodded.

'It has a structural fault and has been declared dangerously unstable. It could come down at any time.'

'All right.'

'Are you hungry? I could bring you some food.'

'Yes, yes, I am.'

'Would a cold chicken sandwich do?'

'That would be fine. Thank you.'

'I'll bring you a Coke to go with it.'

We stopped at a tall, heavy door, which she pushed open, and we entered. Inside the room was a four-poster bed with a mountain of pillows and some furniture in the shadows.

There appeared to be thick drapes over the windows. A fire roared in the fireplace.

'This is your bedchamber,' Misty said, moving into the room.

This was going to be *my* room! I looked at her in a daze. After the cage...

'I'm afraid it is a bit cold. Since there is no electricity we've had to rely on wood logs. Fortunately the chimney was still in working condition. I'll bring some extra blankets and hot water bottles for you later.'

'Thank you,' I said automatically, although I was not cold at all. I was used to much colder weather than this. I followed her into the room, utterly awestruck by my strange and wonderful surroundings.

Misty opened a cupboard. 'All the clothes in here are for you. They were all bought specially for you so they should fit, but if you have any problems just let me know.'

'Oh,' I exclaimed, surprised. There were so many clothes hanging in the wardrobe, and to think that they were all new and mine! I had never had anything new before. All my clothes were hand-me-downs.

She smiled. 'It's a nuisance not having electricity. You won't be able to watch TV tonight. Can you read?'

I nodded.

She flushed. 'I didn't mean to imply that you couldn't read. I really meant to say that all we have here are English books and can you read in English? I was told you were Russian...' she trailed off uncomfortably.

'Yes, I can read English. My mother was once an English teacher in Moscow. A book would be nice.'

I felt her frown mentally. Wondering why an English teacher's daughter had been sold. But all she said was, 'I believe we have some books in our library by Russian authors. I think I've seen Gorky, Ibsen, and Chekhov in the library. I'll find something for you.'

'Thank you.'

She turned away from me and opened a door. 'This is the bathroom.' She showed me into a tiled space and demonstrated how to use the shower. Imagine my surprise when she told me that there was hot and cold water in the taps and that it could be mixed to my satisfaction. There was also a flush toilet and clean towels on a heated railing. 'Well, it will be when the electricity comes back,' she said.

We went out of the bathroom and she gestured toward another door at the opposite end. 'That is a connecting door to what was once a dressing room. There is no one in there, but you can just keep it locked anyway.'

I turned and looked at her. 'So who owns all this?'

'Guy. He is the master and owner of everything you see. He is away now, but you will meet him tomorrow night.'

'I see.' I desperately wanted to ask her more about the man who had bought me, but she averted her eyes and changed the subject abruptly.

'Hopefully the strong winds will be over tonight and power and the telephone lines will be restored by tomorrow. It's simply awful to be without.' She shivered. 'It's so awfully cold.'

I didn't say anything. I had spent my entire life without power.

'I guess that's it, unless you have any questions,' she said.

'May I borrow a safety pin, please?'

'Of course.'

'Thank you.'

When she left I went and sat on the bed, staring at the splendor of my surroundings and thinking about Guy. What would he be like? What kind of a man buys a woman? A part of my brain said a rich man who for some reason could not get a girl through normal means, or a rich man who had neither care nor time for messy emotions.

In an hour Misty was back with a sandwich, a drink, some blankets, two hot water bottles, and a safety pin attached to a piece of cardboard. After she had gone I unpinned the safety pin from the cardboard and very carefully unpicked my mother's lace. I held it close to the lamp and smiled with satisfaction. It was unharmed.

For a while I held it against my cheek and closed my eyes. And I could see my mother's face in the candlelight as if it was yesterday. It was not her fault. I understood it now. She had lost the capacity for hope. My father with his infinite capacity for callousness had ground it out of her. I thought of Nikolai and I prayed that he would be safe. That my father would not break him the way he had broken my mother. Filled with a deep sadness, I took a pillowcase off one of the pillows and carefully wrapping the lace inside put it in the top drawer of the dresser.

All around me the castle was silent and dark, but I was too wound up to sleep. Misty had brought me a book titled, *The Complete Works of Anton Chekhov*. I opened it and started reading *Uncle Vanya* in English. It felt strange to have Marina and Astrov talking English.

Outside, the wind screamed and tore at the wooden shutters.

Chapter 10

Sleeping in the castle that night I found untold pleasure in the rich bedding and softness of the feather pillows. I was both snug and cozy, with lots of blankets and two hot water bottles, but because the building sat on a high chalk plateau the wind really did howl in tempestuous gusts around the walls, turrets, and even wailed down the chimney of my bedroom.

I was abruptly awakened by a loud crack and an almighty crash in the middle of the night. I pulled the blankets in closer about my neck and lay very still to listen to the furious wind bashing the castle. Finally the worst of the storm passed and I fell back into a fitful sleep. I dreamed that a woman in a long green silk dress came to stand at the doorway. She was backlit so I could not see her face.

'Mama?' I called. Why I thought she must be my mother I do not know because she was tall, unlike my petite mother.

She shook her head slowly, sadly.

'Who are you?' I asked.

She shook her head again and vanished.

I woke up disorientated and cold. The fire had gone out and the hot water bottles had gone cold. I got out of bed and pulling the blankets off the bed wrapped myself in them, and went to the window. I pulled open the drapes and the wooden shutters. Dawn was in the sky. I opened the window and inhaled the scent of the rain and damp earth. Though it was a mild day, the cold of the coming winter was already in the air.

The view across the lawns was dreamlike and glorious.

There were no houses as far as the eye could see. Only the wide expanse of wilderness broken by russet-colored woods and in the distance a hill, its slopes filled with heather and bracken. I turned back and looked at my room in the milky light of day.

The walls were a shiny arctic blue, the four-poster bed I had slept in had faded, disintegrating silk embroideries, the floor was dark wood, and there was a large tapestry hanging on one wall. Once it must have been full of emerald greens, reds, and gold, but now it was so in need of a good cleaning that it seemed as though it had been made of shades of gray wool. The furniture consisted of a writing desk, a cupboard, and a chintz chaise-longue.

I could hear the castle starting to wake up with the sound of voices echoing in the vast emptiness.

I used the bathroom quickly. There was no hot water and it was drafty and cold. When I opened the closet in the light of day, I saw that it was filled mostly with thick winter wear. I dressed in a pair of black jeans, a brown blouse, and a thick green sweater. There were three shoeboxes at the bottom of the wardrobe. I sat on my heels and opened them all. A pair of sensible black leather shoes, sturdy walking boots, and white sneakers. I laced the sneakers and got into them. They fit perfectly.

I left the room and walked along the corridor. It was very poorly lit as there was no natural light at all, and the damp and cold came through the walls. It was only when I got to the main staircase that light filtered in through the many slit windows high in the thick walls. Standing at the top of the stairs I got my first real look at the great hall of the house. It was two floors high and absolutely massive. And it was in a terrible state of disrepair.

The fireplace was big enough to roast an ox in, but its breast was blackened with soot. Once people had built their fire in it, stoked it, and held their hands to its blaze. But I guessed that had been a long, long time ago—not years but centuries ago. Some of the torches set against the walls were broken. The crossed swords and the coat of arms were dull with dust. Cobwebs hung from the curved and elaborate Gothic ceiling.

There were many paintings missing from the walls. They had left pale squares and rectangle shapes on the walls. The magnificent checkered yellow and cream stone floor was unpolished. Tapestries of majestic proportions were all moth-eaten and almost beyond any kind of restoration. The carpets were threadbare. It was a crying shame that such a beautiful home had fallen into disgrace in this way.

The only thing that rose out of the despair and neglect of the house was a huge vase full of white lilies. Its fragrance and beauty filled the space and lifted it. From my vantage point I could see light and activity coming from the room beyond the huge lobby of the house.

I went down the intricately carved dark wood stairs. The elk's head mounted on the landing reminded me of my father. How many heads had I seen in my lifetime? How many pairs of glassy eyes? I turned my face away and headed toward the voices and light. It was a saloon. It had fine furniture that had seen better days, worn upholstery, more pale squares and rectangles on the walls, and what looked like a really good grand piano.

Misty was standing in her coat by a large fireplace, her palms spread to the dancing flames, talking to a man in a black suit. Both turned toward me as I hovered at the door.

'Hello, Lena,' Misty greeted. 'Come and meet Mr. Ben Fellowes. It's his job to take care of Guy. He always travels ahead of Guy to make sure that everything is just the way Guy likes it. Mr. Fellowes, this is Lena Seagull. She arrived last night.'

Mr. Fellowes was a thin man with a long, serious face and slate blue eyes. He focused them on me with unsmiling intensity. 'Welcome to Broughton Castle, Miss Seagull,' he said with a formal bow. It was so stiff it was almost a mockery.

'Thank you. Seagull is not really my name. Please call me Lena.'

'Did you sleep well?' asked Misty.

Like a princess in a castle, I wanted to say, but I didn't. 'Yes, thank you.'

'That's good. Mr. Fellowes was just telling me that the storm brought down the three-hundred-year-old beech tree by the chapel cemetery last night.'

'Yes, I think I might have heard it fall during the night,' I said carefully. My English was rusty and I didn't want to make any mistakes.

'When you lose such a tree it is like losing a part of history. Who knows what that tree silently witnessed?'

'It is a terrible shame,' agreed Mr. Fellowes.

Misty sighed and turned toward me. 'Well, the power will be back on this afternoon. The weather is terrible, so you can decide if you just stay in here by the fire and read, or explore the castle. It's in a bad state so you have to be careful where you go. You'll find that in the summer bats roost in the nooks and crannies of the ceiling.'

'Am I allowed to play the piano?'

She frowned. 'I don't think it's tuned. I don't believe anybody has played it for years.'

I felt enthusiastic and happy at the thought of playing again. 'That's all right, I know how to tune a piano.'

She looked at me with surprise. 'Really?'

'Yes, we had to tune our own. It is not very difficult. I haven't snapped a string yet.'

She smiled. 'A girl of many talents then.'

'You don't have the necessary tools. I will get a professional tuner in this afternoon,' Mr. Fellowes injected coldly. 'Have a good day, ladies.' Nodding to both Misty and me he went, his back ramrod straight, like an actor exiting the stage.

'Breakfast will be served in the breakfast room, just through there, in about two hours' time.'

I nodded, still thinking of Mr. Fellowes and his obvious dislike of me. When I turned back Misty was rubbing her hands together. She picked up a small white object and gave it to me. It was a mobile phone. I had seen Timur use one.

'I don't know how to use it,' I said.

'It's really easy. Basically, you have to keep it with you at all times so Guy and I are always able to reach you. If you need to call me I have already put my number in. Just press this button, and then this, and then hit the OK button. Try it.'

I tried it and a ringing came from her pocket. She answered it and said, 'Hello.'

I heard it like an echo in my ear.

She hung up. 'OK?'

'OK,' I said. It seemed easy enough.

'The same way you are never to leave these premises without Guy's consent, you cannot use your phone to have any contact with the outside world.' Her tone had changed, become more official and stern.

'All right,' I agreed immediately.

She put her mobile away and began to rub her hands again.

'Is there a baby or a small child living in this castle?' I asked.

She stopped rubbing her hands and looked at me strangely. 'No, why do you ask?'

'I thought I heard a baby crying last night.'

'That will be the wind.' She grinned. 'Or the ghost.'

'Ghost?'

'Yes, local gossip has it that this castle is haunted. She smiled again to show me that she did not believe a word of the local gossip. 'Legend has it that no woman can ever live here. Each one suffers some tragedy. Over the decades the malevolence has even been felt by anyone simply passing by the large gates. You should ask Mr. Fellowes, he knows all about it.'

'I will,' I said thoughtfully.

'Well, I'd better be off then. I've got work to do. See you at breakfast,' Misty said with a grin and she was gone too. I went to the piano and opened it. It was an exceptionally beautiful instrument. A much sought after French Gaveau. My mother's piano had been an upright Bechstein, but her favorite brand was the Gaveau. How she would have loved to play such a grand and beautiful piano.

I hit middle C and it was so flat that a cat could have lain on it. Mr. Fellowes was right. I had no business tuning such a fine instrument. My thoughts turned to the master of the castle. Guy. I tried the name on my tongue and it slid off smoothly. So he was coming today. I felt nervous. Soon it would be time for me to collect more wretched memories.

At breakfast time I met Mollie, the maid who ran errands and helped the cook. And Ren, the gardener. And of course the cook, Madeline Littlebell. A stern woman who held her nose at a high angle as if there was a bad smell in the room. She had cooked a wonderful breakfast—bacon, fried eggs, sausages, muffin, toast, and something I had never seen before called a croissant. There was jam and honey on the table and as much butter as I wanted.

'You'll never starve here,' Mrs. Littlebell said.

'Don't let Mrs. Littlebell's appearance fool you. She can rival the best French chef,' Misty said.

'How would you know? You hardly eat,' Mrs. Littlebell replied, but she was pleased by the compliment.

Except for Mr. Fellowes who was subtly hostile, everybody else was guardedly friendly as if no one really knew how to treat me. I ate heartily but my real appetite was for more information about the man who had bought me. Still, I could not get Misty alone. She rushed off after eating two lightly buttered slices of toast and before anybody else had finished.

After breakfast I spent the morning in the library. It was another dimly lit cavernous room filled from floor to ceiling with old books. The books were yellowed and filled with silverfish. It was obvious that no one ever came to this room. I dusted off a deep armchair and tried to read, but it was cold and I could not concentrate. Eventually I left and went back to the breakfast room to wait for Misty to show up for lunch.

Fortunately, she arrived before everyone else.

'There you are,' she said with a genuinely friendly smile. 'I was just about to go looking for you.'

'I need to talk to you, Misty.'

'Oh, well, come along to the saloon then.'

We walked together to the saloon and Misty sat on the sofa nearest to the fireplace.

'It's so fucking cold,' she complained. 'Fortunately, it will all come back on in about an hour's time. So what did you want to talk to me about?'

'I just wanted to know more about what is expected of me.'

She frowned. 'Nothing is expected of you.' She licked her lips. 'Other than what you do for Guy at night. He will be flying in by helicopter sometime this afternoon and you will be required to make yourself available for him tonight at nine forty-five. I will come and pick you up and take you to him.'

I nodded. 'OK.'

'Guy has instructed you to wear the dressing gown that you will find laid out on your bed and nothing under it. And please leave your hair loose.'

'Can we talk a little bit about Guy?'

'What do you want to know?'

'Has he fallen on bad times?'

'Goodness no. Guy is a billionaire.'

'Oh!' A billionaire. Even a millionaire was outside my comprehension. I frowned. 'Why the missing paintings then? And why would he allow this beautiful old castle to fall into ruin like this?'

'Broughton Castle is actually a baronial estate that borrows the appearance of a castle. It was built during the Gothic revival. I believe Guy bought it and everything in it without having seen it: what was left of the paintings, the books, the kitchen equipment, the furniture... Everything.'

'Why doesn't he do it up then?'

'I'm afraid I don't know. And even if I did I couldn't discuss it with you. He is very private and anything he wants you to know he will tell you himself.'

'Can you at least describe him to me?'

'The truth is, Lena, nobody here except Mr. Fellowes has actually seen his face. He wears a mask at all times.'

'A mask? Why?' I asked, quite shocked by the information.

Her voice dropped a few octaves. 'He was involved in a car accident. His face was very badly burned and now he will never allow anyone to see him without his mask other than Mr. Fellowes.'

Immediately I thought of an old hunchbacked creature, so ugly that he had to wear a mask at all times. I felt my heart sink. First Zara and her perversions and now this. 'But what's he like?' My tone, I was glad to note, was level and not as unhappy as I felt.

She shrugged. 'He keeps himself to himself, but even masked he is one hell of a man. To start with he has a really sexy, ripped body. He doesn't sleep much and often he trains for hours at night. I once accidentally saw him in the gym. I made the mistake of not showing myself straight away and had to stay hidden behind one of the pillars for two bloody hours! I've never seen anyone push themselves like that. Running, lifting weights, pulling himself up on the bar. Still, lovely body.'

*****

Later that afternoon the power was returned to the castle. The lights came on and heat began to issue out of the wooden boxes attached to the walls. About two hours later I heard the sound of a helicopter arriving and I felt a knot of nervous fear clutch at my stomach. It never left until Misty came to fetch me at exactly nine forty-five p.m.

'Are you ready?' She seemed very solemn.

I nodded apprehensively.

We walked silently in the long bare corridors. It was an unhappy place that appealed to an unhappy man.

She opened a door to a bedroom similar to mine. A large fire burned in the fireplace filling the room with its warmth and light.

I got naked and Misty fit leather straps around my wrists and ankles. When they were snugly bound she hooked them to the chains that were anchored to the posters of the bed. The press of the leather and the rattling of the chains were not foreign. This had already been done to me. I had already been locked in a cage like an animal. No choices. No pleasure. Just my fate.

But then she secured the blindfold over my eyes. And the experience became totally different. With my eyes covered all my senses were heightened and intensified. I quieted my mind and quietly waited for him. The bed beneath my cheek was soft; the sheet was silky and cool. There was a breeze. It must have been coming from the chimney. I started to filter the silence. Muffled footsteps in the corridor. Heavier than Misty's.

My heart started pounding hard. I heard the doorknob turn. The door opened. Someone was standing at the doorway looking in. My pulse jumped. The silence was deafening. Seconds passed. I remained very still, very quiet. Then footsteps. Nearing. I felt his energy. It reached out before him. Like a hand. And touched me.

Chapter 11

Hawke

Stunning. She was stunning. I caught my breath. The firelight danced on her creamy skin and raw, primal desire pulsed in my heated blood.

She had been chained and presented exactly as I had requested. Beautifully. Forehead to the bed, arms stretched out, ass in the fucking air. She lay very still in her shackles except for the imperceptible movement her body made with every breath she took. Her blonde hair fell over the sides of her face, covering it and spreading out on the sheet. Fascinated I watched her skin stretch over her spine and shoulder blades, her buttocks. She was pale and untouched, like a pure angel. I felt a sudden dizzying rush of power. And she was *mine*. My possession. I bought you. I own you, Lena Seagull. You are *mine* to do with as I please.

She was here for my pleasure.

I owned her the way I owned my shoes.

I wanted to bury myself inside her mouth, her cunt, her ass. I wanted to brand the angel. A sudden rush of blood to my cock made it pulse and harden painfully. It felt as if it would rip apart with the intense pressure of my arousal. It was begging for release. I took pleasure in the pain. It was a long time since it had done that. I took a deep breath. I would use her as if she was an object existing purely for my pleasure. I never wanted to know one fucking thing about her or her miserable little life, or her inevitably sad story.

I would only ever see her in this room in this magnificent position. I would never look into her eyes. I would never lose control. I would never allow myself to be weak. She was here for MY pleasure and mine alone.

I moved into the room and stood at the back of her. Her plump ass was held high in the air, the puckered hole ready for me to enter it. Between the cheeks her cunt, plump and pink and juicy, pushed up as if begging for my cock to drive into it. I wanted to grab her hair and pound her so hard with my cock that she screamed. I wanted to see her writhe under me.

I walked up to her, my eyes riveted by the wet heat I saw glistening at the center of her. I stood over her. She had begun to shake with fear. The air felt thick with her anxiety.

'Lift your ass.'

Her body slid backward and downward as her ass moved up toward me. I put the tip of my finger on the entrance to her sex. Her instinctive reaction was to jump away, but she stilled it and I inserted my finger about an inch deep. Helplessly, she tensed around it, the tight muscles clenching, and I smiled. I pushed my finger all the way and she gasped. The sound was like that first thrilling note of a symphony orchestra that shimmers in the air above your head. I was maestro of this concert. I reveled in the ultimate power I held over her. She would just be a body, to be taken and ridden, a repository for my sperm. No bullshit feeling or emotions.

I took my finger out of the folds of flesh and went around to the front of her. Her forehead was resting on the bed. I unbuttoned my trousers and pulled the zipper down. I stepped out of my boxers and my cock jumped out eagerly. Kneeling in front of her I fisted the golden mane and pulled her face upwards. She was wearing the blindfold and yet I felt it again. That strange connection. I felt terror. No, a voice inside me cautioned. No. I will not allow this slip of a girl to...defeat me, ruin me. I forced that cold sensation of control to return. It covered me like a cloak. My cock became rock hard.

'You are here to be mine...in every possible way. When I tell you to do something, you must do it instantly. You are not to challenge me in any way. Is that understood?'

My answer was a slight tightening of her hair in my fist.

'Open your mouth. I want to fuck that first.' My voice was unforgiving and stern.

Without hesitation, like a blind newborn creature that turns its face toward a nourishing breast, she opened her mouth, her lips trembling.

Fuck. Why did she cause this reaction in me? She was nothing. Just a piece of meat. I would use her and discard her.

Angry with myself I shoved my cock roughly into her open mouth. Her lips closed lightly around the engorged head. The inside of her mouth was warm and silky. She didn't do anything, simply held me inside the wet heat as I had instructed her to. It didn't feel right. Nothing felt right.

'Tighter,' I ordered harshly.

She wrapped her lips so tightly her cheeks hollowed. Desire raced through my body. Holding onto her hair, I plunged into her mouth, faster, deeper, harder until she was choking and gagging and struggling with the full size of my cock, but I did not stop. Her lips and tongue rolled over my skin. Gripping her hair hard I exploded inside her mouth. Her body jerked with surprise.

'Don't swallow. Open your mouth and show me.'

I slid easily out of her.

She held her mouth open with her throat closed and I saw my seed swirling inside her mouth. It gave me a cheap thrill.

'Now swallow,' I instructed.

She closed her mouth and swallowed.

'Lick your lips.'

A pink tongue snaked out and licked the remaining drops of semen. Her absolute obedience did not bring satisfaction or pleasure. It disturbed me. I stared at her curiously. She was a well-trained girl. Training like that must take a hefty dose of fear. The thought made me frown.

I let her hair go, but her face remained unmoving and in the position I had held it in, the throat exposed and stretched. I noticed that her blindfold had become darker with tears.

Like a man in a daze I reached out a hand, and nearly touched the wet blindfold, before I remembered myself, and retracted it quickly. Damn her. The tenacity was admirable, but I would not allow that admiration to grow into anything more. Allowing emotion to creep into my heart would mean losing control... To her. She would never have such power over me. I would never allow it. I pushed away from her and went around her to her raised ass.

'Spread your legs.'

She spread them rather well. Her submission gave me pleasure, but as if to make a point I dug my fingers into the soft flesh of her thighs and spread them farther so that every part of her was exposed to me and she was in an unnatural and humiliating position. Without warning I pushed my finger into her little pussy. The muscles rippled around my finger as I curled it and massaged the secret wall of flesh inside her. I heard her indrawn breath and increased my speed until she was dripping onto my hand. She never made a sound.

I grabbed her hips and holding them up so her knees no longer touched the mattress I pushed into her glistening whorls of flesh slowly. She was so small and tight I had to force my way in. Her body was shuddering as she stretched to accommodate the size of my cock, and yet she made not a whimper or a moan. She did not try to beg her way out of it or act innocent or manipulate me with tears. I tried to ignore her complete silence, but it stung me. It made me rough. I plunged in. The mattress sank with the force of my thrust.

She gasped. I luxuriated in the reaction.

There was still an inch to go. I wanted to possess her completely. I wanted her to be completely taken. I wanted to see her writhing at the end of my cock. I drove in and buried myself to the hilt. Her body tried to jerk away, but my fingers were digging into her flesh and holding her so tightly that no movement was possible. She made a small stifled sound. I knew that I had hurt her then.

It was barely a gasp but I heard it, and it pained me as if I had hurt myself. And that surprised me. I had never been big on empathy. Money. That was the language and emotion I understood. She had one job and one job only. To service me. To be available to me whenever I wanted her to be a wild animal that I had to tame. I wanted her to thrash out, so that when I took her hair in my fist I would not care if I hurt her.

She gasped. It gave me goose bumps. Her thighs began to tremble. I watched her body tremble as she took in deep breaths. I waited for her to accommodate my width and length and then I began to ram into her hard. In and out. In, out. Savagely, like a man possessed, and perhaps I was that, that night. I pumped into her virgin cunt with a ruthlessness that I would not have thought myself capable of. Her slim body jerked under the brutal assault. Sweat gleamed on her skin.

It was wrong. I knew it was wrong and the knowledge made me even more ruthless. She was already getting the better of me. The slap of my skin against her was loud in the empty room. I grunted with the force of my thrusts. Her tight muscles contracted involuntarily and milked me of everything I had.

My climax was powerful and hard. I roared, bucked, and, with heat radiating out of me, exploded deep inside her. For a moment I remained kneeling on the bed, gripping her hips hard, and buried deep inside and spilling the last bit of my seed into her.

Then I pulled out of her. I saw her blood and I felt *victorious*. The delicate skin of her sex was torn. I had branded her. She will never forget me for as long as she lives. She will be an old woman in a rocking chair and she will remember this night. I stared at her cunt. It looked swollen and used. She lay unmoving.

I put out a hand and began to play with her folds. Smearing our juices and playing with that hidden bud. I felt her body tense. The involuntary response fired my blood the way that most seductive women had not. It raced in my veins. I was ready to take her again, but I did not. I knew she could not take it. I circled the bud the way the predator does its prey. Slowly, with total focus.

She climaxed like no other woman I knew. A fierce growl rose in her throat. Her skin flushed a rosy pink and her body and sex convulsed sharply. Her toes pointed involuntarily. Her cry was muffled: she had bitten the mattress. She was breathing hard when I stood up and got dressed. She remained in her position and I walked to the door. When I touched the handle she spoke for the first time. And the sound of her voice, young and sweet and clear, was like a knife. It cut me to the bone.

'Is this going to be my life from now on?' she asked, her voice ringing out as clear as a bell.

I turned and looked at her, and her blindfolded face was turned in my direction. Blonde hair streamed down her neck and shoulders. Some strands were damp and stuck to her forehead and cheeks. She must have bitten her lip; it was bleeding. I had used her and abused her. With blood running from her mouth and vagina, she looked totally helpless, soiled, and pitiful, and yet in that moment I saw her not from my position of master at the doorway to her abuse, but from the wilderness of my soul, and she seemed a light, pure and shining. It was I who was unclean and contemptible. The thick scars on my face burned. Time had been heavy on my soul.

I realized then that I would never win this game. I would never reign over her.

In fact, I had already lost. Without even having seen her gray eyes. Saying nothing I opened the door and walked out of the room. Ceba had heard my approach, and was already on his feet. I touched his blameless head. The soft fur. A strange feeling swept over me. I recognized it suddenly. Intense guilt. I was harming her. The feeling that I had betrayed her. I was connected to her somehow. And angry with myself. I could have done it in a different way. It was not her fault. Her complete stillness had shocked me. Her total lack of emotion.

I took out my mobile and called Misty.

'I'm finished,' I said. My voice was cold and distant, but inside me I was in a state of terrible turmoil. Her blood was on my hands and body. I needed a shower. I needed to wash away my shame.

Chapter 12

Lena

The door closed and I heard his footsteps disappear down the corridor. For a little while there was silence. I moved my cramped body until I lay curled up on my side. The chains rattled. My mind was blank. Perhaps I was in shock. I felt removed from the room, from what had just happened to me. I felt lost and confused. As if I had just woken up from a dream. I grasped a fistful of the sheet underneath me and gripped it tight as if it could keep me from tumbling into the abyss.

The past seemed so far away. So lost. The memories so distant that they could be visited only in my dreams.

I knew I had been sold to be a sexual object for someone's use, but I had acknowledged it only vaguely, and carefully had never given the picture detail or color. In truth I had never imagined that this is what it would come to. Chained and sexually abused by a stranger I would never see.

I knew he was tall. I could tell by the height his voice was coming from. He had big hands and a big penis. It had hurt me. I heard a sound in the corridor. Then the door opened and I heard Misty gasp from the doorway. Her steps toward me were light and quick. She removed the blindfold.

'He hurt you. You're bleeding,' she said. There was anger in her voice.

Even more than the shame I felt about a total stranger having put his sexual organ into me and done whatever he pleased with me, I felt ashamed and humiliated that she should see me in this way. I shook my head.

'It doesn't matter,' I mumbled.

But she was furious. 'Oh, you poor thing,' she ranted. 'He's a bastard. I used to admire him and think he was special, and now I can see that he is just a monster.'

The angrier she became on my behalf, the sadder and smaller I felt. 'Free me, please,' I said, my voice trembling with shame and confusion.

Immediately she set about releasing me. I rubbed my skin where the leather had left red marks. Misty held out my gown and I quickly covered my nakedness. I tied the sash at my waist and forced myself to meet her eyes. They were pitying. 'Come,' she said. 'I'll take you to your room.'

I would not have pity from anyone. I raised my chin. 'No, I know the way. Please go back to bed. I'll be fine. I just need to be alone.'

'All right, if you are sure.'

'Yes.'

'Goodnight then.'

She turned and walked toward the door.

'Misty?'

'Yes?'

'Thank you.'

I stood watching the fire and listening to her footsteps fade. Then I glanced at the bed, the shackles, the blood-smeared sheet. Going to the bed I ripped the sheet off and bundled it. I held it pressed against my stomach and felt cold and alone. I dropped it on the bed and walked to the window, and, pulling aside the disintegrating velvet curtains, looked out. It was a still night with a large, low moon in the sky.

I hugged myself and thought about my life. How long would I have to be here? I had to find a way to make him talk to me. I had to find a way to persuade him to bring my brother into this country. I had nothing I could use other than my body. So be it. In the reflection of the windowpane I saw myself. I appeared white and sad. Slowly, I let the dressing gown drop and watched myself in the glass. I looked at the ghostly reflection of myself until I was so cold my goose bumps scattered my body. I picked up my dressing gown and put it back on. My body ached.

I turned away from the window and, leaving the room, walked toward my bedroom at the end of the next wing. In my bedroom I took off the gown and stood under the spray of a hot shower. I touched myself between my legs curiously. My flesh felt sore and sensitive.

I thought of him. How acutely aware I had been of him. I had heard nothing and no one, and sensed nothing but his every move and sound. He had commanded my entire attention.

He must be very strong. I remembered that when he had first entered my body the pain was so sharp it was like being stabbed and I had instinctively jumped away from him, but his powerful hands had tightened on my hips and held me so powerfully that I could move not even an inch while he had slowly filled me up. The sensation of being full and stretched was so foreign.

Maybe I was shocked that he had made me climax. The woman had tried until I was sore and she had never managed. Eventually I had learned to pretend. To make my body go rigid and to moan the way she did. It seemed to satisfy and please her.

I remembered again the way my orgasm had overtaken my body. So powerfully that I had been afraid that something horrible was happening to me. I had opened my mouth to shout out in fear when the sensation of falling away was suddenly replaced by an intense and indescribable pleasure I had never experienced before. Then hot lights behind my eyelids and my heart fluttering like a bird in distress. It had shocked me to the core.

I got out of the shower and rubbed myself with a towel and noticed the bluish-black finger marks Guy had left on my hips and thighs. They did not hurt. I let the dressing gown slide to the floor. In the mirror I saw that my mouth was swollen. I dressed in my nightgown, lay on the bed, and fell asleep almost immediately. As I slept, right at the edge of my awareness, I sensed someone come into the room and stand over me.

Chapter 13

I had slept badly, again hearing the baby crying and the woman weeping, and woke up early. The storm was well and truly over. I stretched and realized that I was still sore between my legs, but I was full of curiosity about my surroundings. I rolled out of bed and headed for the bathroom. Weak sunshine filtered in through the tiny windows, but it was lovely and warm and I stood for a long time under a blissfully hot shower. Just as I had finished my toilette there was a knock on the door and Misty walked in.

'Are you all right?' she asked.

'Yes, I'm fine.' I released my hair from its topknot.

But she carried on looking at me anxiously, as if I was suffering from something terminal.

'Don't worry, I'm really all right,' I said, with a confident smile.

She smiled back. 'I was worried about you. You looked bad last night.'

'I'm good this morning,' I said very firmly. Pity I did not want. From anybody.

'You know that I have to take you to the room again tonight?'

I shrugged nonchalantly. 'Of course.'

'Right. See you at breakfast.'

I got dressed and went downstairs. There were voices and sounds coming from the breakfast room, but even though I was ravenously hungry, I didn't want to see anybody so I slipped out of the front door and went for a walk.

The air was crisp and it felt good to be outdoors again. But the same disrepair that was inside the house was reflected outside. Statues covered in lichen and moss, water features choked in weeds, and a rose arbor that was so wild and full of brambles and thorns that it was not possible to walk under it. It was sad.

I walked up to the tree that had come down in the storm. It was very pitiful. I tried to imagine what the tree might have seen in its lifetime of more than three hundred years and could not. I kept on walking until I came to a Gothic chapel cemetery. The door was locked so I could not go in.

By the time I went back it was nearly two. I had missed lunch and I was hungry, but there was no one around in the breakfast room. I didn't dare go down to the kitchen because I didn't think Mrs. Littlebell would appreciate it. In fact the entire castle seemed deserted and silent except for the ticking of the grandfather clock by the main staircase. I wondered where Guy was and what he was doing. Or what Misty actually did for Guy.

In my room I found a ham and salad sandwich rolled up in paper and a Thermos flask of hot chocolate on a tray. There was a note from Misty saying that there was a coffee machine in the breakfast room that was kept on all day and I should help myself if I wanted any.

Carefully, I took the meat out of the sandwich and wrapped it up in the paper the sandwich had come in. Then I sat on the bed and ate the meatless sandwich. I finished the hot drink and thought about going downstairs to see if Misty was about, but I must have been more tired than I thought because I fell asleep. By the time I woke up it was already dark outside.

I switched on the lights and went downstairs to the saloon. Misty looked up from some papers. 'Hello, you'll be pleased to know that the piano has been tuned.'

'Good,' I said.

'Will you play something for me?'

I went to the piano and opened it. The smell had changed. I closed my eyes for a moment. Memories flooded my brain. Tears came to my eyes. I opened my eyes, and damn it, but water started to leak from them. I didn't want Misty to know that I was crying so I didn't wipe them away. They flowed down my cheeks and dripped onto my jeans while I played. It was an old, sad song that my mother had taught me.

When I had finished Misty stood from her chair and came to me.

She was holding a box of tissues. 'You really are very good. I don't think I have ever heard anyone play so well outside of a concert.'

I pulled out a couple of tissues and wiped my face and blew my nose. 'Thank you.'

'Don't forget I have to take you to see Guy again tonight.' Her eyes slid away from mine.

As if it was something I could forget. 'Of course. What time?'

'Same as yesterday.'

I nodded.

*****

Misty came for me at nine forty-five p.m. I was waiting for her on the bed. She knocked and I stood from the bed and followed her down the corridor back to the room. I went to the bed and took my dressing gown off.

'Lie on your back in the middle of the bed,' Misty told me.

I did as she asked.

'Open your legs a little.'

I flushed with embarrassment, but I did as I was asked. She put the leather restraints on my ankles and chained them to the bedposts. Then she did my wrists. After securely blindfolding me she left. After she had gone I tested my hands and legs. I could only curl my hands some, but I still had a lot of movement in my legs. I took a deep breath and waited.

Soon I heard his step in the corridor. I heard him open the door and pause there. He came farther into the room and circled me like a predator. I sensed it—the power and the sheer strength of him. It was a long, torturous time before I heard him again.

'Spread your legs.'

Heat licked my skin as I moved my legs farther apart.

'Bend your knees and let your legs drop open sideways.'

More movement. This time closer. I felt his hand on my shoulder and I jumped. A bolt of electrified energy like I had never known rattled through my body and made my hair stand on end. It was so powerful he could not have not felt it too. He removed his hand and the room became deathly quiet. But the silence was not empty. In it lived danger, desire: his and...mine. The excitement emanated out of his body in strong waves that were almost physical in nature.

The mattress gave way. Again I had the impression of a very large man. I felt hot breath on my skin, then the tender brush of lips on my neck, burning as they made contact with my flesh. I smelt wine and spices. A decadent, exotic, old world smell. Fingertips trailed down my body. A wave of pure pleasure ran through my entire body. My sex throbbed with need.

A hand ran through my hair, butterfly kisses burnt a trail down to my shoulders, my hair, lower down to my chest, on my breast, and then his wet hot mouth took my nipple into it. My breath escaped in a rush. The sensation was a tingling... A warning.

You cannot resist this.

My belly clenched with the fire in it. Between my legs I became wet with thick juices. I had never felt like this before. The woman had tried everything. Her fingers, her tongue... Nothing had moved me. My body— the meat and bones that I was—arched on its own. No matter what the logical part of my brain thought, my body wanted to *submit* to this man. It was begging for him to take me.

'That's right,' he encouraged; the words were low and base, as if they had come from somewhere deep within him.

A large hand landed on my waist, firm and totally in control. His leg slid between mine and his knee, hard and hot, pressed into my sodden center. I could not help it, my bones felt as if they were melting. I lost my head. My hand came up to touch him. It was only tentative, weak, unformed, a gesture just born out of lust, but it stilled him like a bucket of cold water on a pair of mating dogs.

I felt his teeth on my nipple and his hands shove between my legs and grip me viciously. I went limp, like those insects that play dead when you poke them with a stick. I didn't know why, but I knew instinctively that I should.

He let go of my nipple but not my sex. 'You are here to be touched, not to touch,' he ground out.

Gravity grabbed hold. I no longer flew. I felt myself drop and curl with shame. I wanted to huddle and hide myself. But I couldn't. My body was splayed open. My most intimate area exposed and his to do with as he pleased. My limbs felt heavy. A starfish in the mid-sun.

I nodded. It would never be the same again.

He moved so that his bulge pressed between my legs. Trapped under him a spark deep within caught fire. My body started to flush. I felt his body move, the muscles coiling. Then he was blowing on my open, exposed sex. My breasts heaved with my quickening breaths. My sex blossomed with heat, grew, opened up to welcome him.

Without warning his silky mouth was on that little bud of my sex. My body arched uncontrollably and I gasped out loud. Lazily he swiped his tongue along the entire pulsing crack as I shivered with a strange need. I wanted him. I wanted him deep inside. Like last night.

He inserted a finger into me and wriggled it around. 'You are too tight, but in the next few weeks I will use you and stretch you until having my cock inside you becomes the most comfortable thing you can imagine.'

One finger became two and my body strained against the leather restraints.

I felt his ridged abdomen brush against my stomach as he rubbed his hard length along my soaked slit. Then he placed his great erection at the center of me and threaded it into me. The pain was sharp and stabbing, as he forced me to accept his massive, swollen cock. My head pressed back into the pillow and my body shuddered as I opened my muscles and willed the silky hardness in. The thick, mushroomed head of his erection buried itself deeper still into my flesh. Until I was stretched to bursting. No more was possible.

'Ohhhh...'

'Did you think about this today?' he growled harshly.

'Yes.'

'Did you want it?'

I felt him push against the wall. 'Yes.'

'Who's your master, Lena?'

'You.' And at that moment it was as if my brain had been reprogrammed, overridden. All thoughts had been deleted and replaced only with the feel of his skin, the sound of his voice, the need to have him inside me.

He laughed, the sound rich and full of satisfaction.

And then he went for it. Ramming into me. Hard. Like a bull. Blindly. Again and again. My body jerked with the force and power in his thrusts. A bead of sweat landed on my stomach. In the darkness I heard the guttural groan of his climax as his body shuddered and he pushed even deeper. I ate that last pain even though it was like a fist inside me. He blasted deep within me. Filled me with his hot seed.

For a long while he lay on my body. Then he withdrew and I felt his eyes on my exposed arousal. I felt his seed leaking out of me. Using only his fingers he rubbed the folds of my sex softly, smearing our juices. The barest contact. It was frustrating. I wanted to grind my hips into his hand. The torment was unbearable. I felt desperate for his touch. My hips jerked into his hand. The wet hunger would not be denied.

'Do you want satisfaction?' he asked.

'Yes,' I whispered instantly.

His fingers began to play with my sex, strumming it like a guitar. Then hard, fast little circles. In seconds it became too much, and that thing that had been building inside me spilled over and I began to spiral into the dizzy pleasure that was more vast than anything I had ever known. A low growl emitted from my lips. Feral. Insatiable.

I rushed toward its violent nature, not caring if I drowned in it or was lost or hurt inside it. It raked me from the top of my head to the tips of my fingers and toes. The other side took me apart and when it returned me I was not quite the same woman that had gone so willingly into it. For a while we were both still and silent. Connected on some mysterious level that neither of us could deny.

'The answer to the question you asked yesterday is simple. You are mine. You will always be mine and only mine. And while I am alive you will never have another man in your body.'

Then I felt cold air where his body had touched mine. I heard the rustle of clothes as he picked them off the floor and dressed.

'Please cover me before you go,' I begged.

I heard him pick up my dressing gown from the table where Misty had left it and bring it to me. I waited until he spread the material on my body and when I felt sure enough of his position I shot my hand out and caught his wrist, the chains rattling. I was being disobedient, standing at the edge of his displeasure, my hold tenuous.

I imagined him looking down at me, surprised, frowning.

'When I was young,' I began, 'my mother told the story of a very poor man who found an injured crane. He took it home and nursed it back to health. After he released it a beautiful woman appeared on his doorstep. He fell in love with her and married her. She told him that she could weave wondrous clothes of the finest silk that he could sell at the market, but he must promise never to watch her making them. She made the clothes and the man became rich by selling them. He asked her to weave more and more, even though it was obvious that her health was declining. In his greed to see her secret so he could reproduce it in some other way he peaked at her while she was weaving. To his shock, he saw a crane plucking feathers from her own body and weaving them into the loom. The crane turned to look at him with sad eyes. Then it flew away never to return.'

I paused.

'The story affected me deeply. I am not like that greedy man. I would never peek. You don't have to chain me. I would never take my blindfold off.'

I released his hand and he stood for a long while over me, watching me. Then he left as quietly as he had come.

Chapter 14

Even though the bed was soft and warm I had slept badly. Again I had dreamed of the woman in green. She had stood at the doorway desolate, mournful, and lonely. Somewhere in the castle a baby was crying.

'What's the matter?' I asked her.

'I'm waiting for her,' she said and disappeared.

I woke up with a start. My room seemed unnaturally cold. I had pushed the blankets away in my sleep and the cold had seeped into my skin. I shivered and pulled them around me. It was five in the morning and the castle was quiet. I wondered what Nikolai would be doing. It was probably not even morning for him. I tried to imagine him in the log cabin and the images felt old and distant. I must find a way to keep my promise.

I lay on the bed and thought about Guy. About the way he made me feel. I touched myself, just on the bed the way he had. A frisson of desire ran through my body. It felt good. I realized that I knew so little about my own body. I did the same things he had done to me and eventually the climax came, but it was not as mind-blowingly explosive as it was with him.

I got out of bed. I planned to walk to the cemetery. I had only seen it in passing while trying the door of the chapel. It was a spooky place and I had not lingered yesterday, but for some unexplainable reason I wanted to read the headstones. I got dressed quickly in warm clothes and my walking boots and set out early. A walk before breakfast would do me good, clear my head. It was a chilly day. There was no wind or clouds, just sub-zero temperatures. There were ice crystals sparkling on the road. My breath rose in visible puffs.

I turned off the tarmac and took the gravel path that led to a bridge over a stream and into a field of rocks and brown-tinged wild grasses that edged the marshy wood. Eventually I came upon a moss-covered, crumbling stone cemetery where various Dufferins with important-sounding titles were buried. Some were so old the etchings were faded. It was overgrown and unkempt. I skirted around a mosaic of leaves stained with gold, orange, red, and brown, and stood at the edge of it wondering what I was really doing there.

A simple, old gray marble stone under a yew tree caught my eye. I walked up to it.

Here lies my child,
Marian Ella Dufferin.
1821–1822
I will not rest until my heart

is cut out from my cold body and
interred inside her little chest of frigid bones.

It began to drizzle but I stood for a long
time mesmerized by the gruesome request. I
tried to imagine such a blind, unthinking love.
My mother never loved us like that. I slid my
hand along the cold marble. Tomorrow I
decided I would come back and tidy up the
grave, pull out the weeds.

My hair was soaked by the time I reached
the castle. It was enshrouded in mist and I felt
again the sense of eerie sadness. The stones
had absorbed it and radiated it.

I went up to my room, dried my hair,
changed into warm clothes, and went to the
breakfast room. Mrs. Littlebell nodded to me.
She seemed to have thawed toward me. When
I slid a piece of bacon into a napkin she saw
me, but quickly averted her eyes.

I hung around until Misty arrived. She
smiled at me.

'How are you this morning? I saw you up
and about so early.'

'Yeah, I went for a walk to the cemetery.'

She picked up a plate and helped herself to
two sausages. 'How morbid. Why?'

'I was curious about the history of this
place. And I saw a really interesting baby's
grave. Do you know anything about it?'

'Well, that will be Countess Isabella Thorn
Dufferin's child. Supposedly her ghost is
unable to rest in peace because she wanted

her heart to be buried with her child and her husband refused to allow it.' Misty turned her face toward the window. Great big drops of rain were running down the glass like fat slime. 'God! Another fucking rainy day.' She plonked down her plate, now also with two slices of toast, and sat. 'What will you do today?'

'I don't know. Maybe I'll explore the castle.'

'Have fun... Just so long as you keep away from the Lady Anne tower.'

As I was leaving the breakfast room Mrs. Littlebell hurried toward me. She had a little package in her hand. She gave it to me.

'This is his favorite—black pudding, made from pig's blood.'

I took it from her gratefully. 'Thank you.'

*****

That afternoon I found the grotto. I had never seen anything like it before and I was fascinated. A room made totally from thousands and thousands of shells pushed into soft cement. There were mermaids carved into the wall and an old man with a long beard. Was he Neptune? The old man of the sea? My mother had told me about him. When I was leaving it I came across Ceba. He stopped and stared at me. I put the bacon and the black pudding on the ground and walked away in the other direction. When I was about twenty yards away I saw him standing by the food looking at me.

'I'm not scared of you. I'll get you yet, Ceba,' I said softly to myself.

*****

Then it was nine forty and I was sitting on my bed naked but for my dressing gown, swinging my foot and listening to the sound of my slipper hissing against the floor. I realized that I was impatient for her to come. I *wanted* to go to him.

Misty arrived at nine forty-five. There was a strange expression on her face.

'What?' I asked her.

'Nothing,' she said and smiled.

We walked together to the room. Inside the room she turned to me. 'Kneel on the bed.'

I knelt on the bed and folded my legs underneath me.

'I am not going to bind you today, only blindfold you.' She picked up the blindfold and held it in front of my eyes. 'You will not remove your blindfold for any reason whatsoever? Is that understood?'

'Yes.'

She secured the covering firmly around my eyes.

'Please remain in this position until he comes.'

'I will,' I said softly, but in fact, my heart was soaring. It was a small victory, but it was an important concession. I would not be chained like an animal.

I listened to her footsteps die away and waited until I heard his. Now that I was not so nervous I could hear that he was not alone. Ceba was with him—his nails clicked on the wooden floor. Guy opened the door and came in alone. I heard the weight of Ceba dropping to the ground.

The door closed.

Slowly, I leaned forward until my bum was in the air and my nose touched the sheet. I inhaled the fragrance of citrus. I turned my face and laid on my cheek. I heard him come forward and stop in front of me. For a few seconds he did nothing, and the muscles of my sex contracted with anticipation. Then the mattress behind me gave way to his weight and I felt warm, strong hands grab my hips. His palms were so big they almost went all the way around my girth.

Without warning he swiped his tongue along my exposed slit with a long, lingering stroke. A small sound of pure pleasure escaped me. My thighs began to quiver as wet heat gathered between my legs.

He lifted his head.

'You have a beautiful pussy.'

I frowned. Pussy must be slang. I had never even considered the idea that my sex could be beautiful. Surely everybody's was the same.

As if he had heard my thoughts he elaborated. 'Pink and fleshy and pouting like a spoilt child... And so fucking wet. You have a pussy that begs to be fucked,' he said and inserted a finger into my sex and then two. He was stretching me again.

I swallowed with the sensations his stroking was producing inside my body.

'Look at you. You're dripping all over my hand. There is only one thing about you I don't like.'

I said nothing.

'Ask me what.'

'What?' I whispered.

'I don't like it that you are silent. Today when you come I want you to scream loudly and hard. I want you to wake the dead with your screams. Can you do that?'

He didn't know that I had been reared in silence. I nodded.

'A yes would have been better.'

'Yes.'

He reached to my nape and gathered my hair in a bundle. With a gentle but firm grip he twirled it in his fist as if it was the finest silk that was running through his hands... And pulled. That way he brought me back to my knees and arched my body backwards. I felt him move, and sensed that his chest was massive, brawny, and full of muscles as it flashed around me before his lips covered the tip of my breast. I bit my lip as my nipple hardened inside the warm wet cave of his mouth. He removed the cave.

'Don't just bite your lip—moan, gasp, whimper, or say my name,' he said softly.

I swallowed.

He sucked my nipple, hard. And this time I let myself go. I made a small sound that was totally foreign to me. Almost like an animal sound. When he left my nipple he pulled his head back and I felt his eyes on the tip as it hardened even more, as if it was yearning for the return of its warm cave. I pushed my chest out toward him.

'My impatient one,' he murmured softly and ran his palm over the over-sensitized tip.

My neck lengthened. My juices ran down my legs. 'Ahhh...'

'That's better,' he encouraged and ran his tongue along my exposed neck. By now I was aching for satisfaction. Aching to be filled by him. Still holding onto my hair he ran the four fingers of his other hand along my throbbing crack as I shivered with pleasure. It was too much and yet not enough. I stiffened with need. He brought those slick fingers to my lips and smeared my own juices on them.

'Open,' he instructed.

I opened my mouth and he slipped his fingers in.

'Suck.'

I closed my lips around his fingers and sucked them. They tasted funny—not disagreeable but different from anything else I had ever tasted.

'You've never tasted yourself, have you?'

I shook my head.

He came really close to my ear. 'Do you like the taste?'

I blushed and he laughed.

'I love the way you taste,' he said, and disentangling his hold on my hair he pushed me back on the pillow. He spread my legs until they were wide open and kissed me gently right in the center of my pussy. For a second I was shocked by the gentle kiss. I felt my heart soar recklessly. This was not sex. This was something more. Then I felt him freeze suddenly.

'You have a very, very beautiful pussy, but what I really want is not cuddles and softness—' he said and using his thumb and fingers parted my soaking wet folds, 'is this.' He thrust into me so suddenly and with such unexpected force and brutality that the breath was knocked out of my lungs. 'And this.'

I gasped for my next breath and clawed the sheet.

'I'm *never* going to fall for your innocent, butter-wouldn't-melt mouth or your greedy little pussy.' He plunged in again. Very hard.

I whimpered.

'The only thing you can ever be is my blindfolded bitch.'

He slammed into me with such force that the bedsprings screeched, my head lifted completely off the pillow, and my entire body slid away in a rush. 'And this is what you will get every day. A good hard fuck in the orifice of my choosing.'

The words were ugly, and I suddenly knew why he had frozen after the gentle kiss. He had remembered that he must not be kind to me, I was just a piece of meat. I should have been hurt or at the very least insulted, but I was too strangely excited by the hot, hard flesh buried deep inside me to care. No matter how much he wanted not to care, there was something between us. It was thick and strong and undeniable.

Shamelessly, I pushed my hips toward him. I didn't want it to stop And it didn't. Again and again I was filled with his cock and fucked until... Ah... My body began to flood with delicious sensation. I felt my eyes roll back in my head with waves of ecstasy, and this time I didn't hold back—the sound that came out of my mouth was his name.

I screamed his name.

Chapter 15

It was raining the next day so I played the piano in the morning and afterwards I spent the day in the library. It was unheated so it was cold and musty smelling but I kind of enjoyed being surrounded by thousands of books. Ever since we were young my mother had instilled a great love for books in us. I dusted off old tomes. Some of them were full of mildew and silverfish. But I found a book I liked—*The God of Small Things* by Arundati Roy. I took it down and went to read it in the saloon. Misty was there.

'Hi,' I said.

'Hi,' she said and smiled tightly.

'What's the matter?'

'Nothing. Just work problems. Anyway, you are requested to join Guy for dinner tonight in the dining room. Dinner will be served at eight p.m., but please go earlier so you don't keep him waiting.'

I stared at her with surprise. 'Guy wants me to have dinner with him?'

'Yes. As usual Mr. Fellowes will serve. Do you know where the dining room is?'

'Yes, I've been in it.'

'Good.' And she smiled again, but uneasily.

*****

I dressed in a black shirt, a pair of black trousers, and the sensible black shoes. Then I brushed my hair until it shone. I looked in the mirror. I looked pale and colorless. I bit my lip to redden it and pinched my cheeks. Then I went down the stairs. The flowers in the huge vase had been changed. The whole place was lifted with the fragrance of lilies. The grandfather clock said that it was seven forty-five. Mr. Fellowes was already there, dressed in his customary gravedigger suit. He nodded formally toward me. His eyes were purposely blank but I felt the curiosity in his gaze.

'Come in, Lena,' he said. I walked into the red room with the long table that could seat sixteen. It had been set for two. There were logs burning in the fireplace.

Mr. Fellowes pointed toward the chair that was beside the head of the table. 'That is your place.'

I walked to it and sat on the leather chair. Then I looked up at Mr. Fellowes and said, 'Will you teach me how to use all these utensils? I have never used anything but a fork and knife.'

Something flashed in Mr. Fellowes' eyes that he quickly suppressed. He came around and stood beside me. Gravely and patiently he taught me about soup spoons, butter knives, side plates, working in from the outside, bread never being cut with a knife, the best place for the napkin being in your lap, and the four o'clock position that knives and forks must be placed in on the plate to signify that one is finished eating.

He coughed politely and looked at his watch.

'Nearly eight?'

'I'm afraid so.'

'Isn't this so strange, Mr. Fellowes?'

He frowned and stiffened. 'You'll never find a kinder man than your master,' he said.

I stared at him, surprised by the loyalty and passion in his voice.

'Thank you, Mr. Fellowes.'

'Not at all,' he replied formally, and stepped back to wait by the sideboard. I felt nervous energy coil in my belly. I clasped my hands in my lap and took a deep breath. A few minutes later I heard steps and the clicking of Ceba's nails on the stone tiles.

The door opened and he stood in the doorway. I had guessed that he was big, but he was taller and broader than I had imagined. That raw prowling energy rushed ahead of him and touched me like a finger. Misty's words flashed into my mind—a masked man projects mystery and ancient allure.

His mask, made out of some malleable material, was skin-colored, and left exposed only his hair—raven black, rakishly long, carelessly styled, and curling at his collar; his mouth, his lips, lush and beautiful; and...his eyes.

I felt as if I had been kicked in the gut!

My heart was thumping so hard I heard the blood roaring in my ears. Unable to tear my eyes away I gazed at him in a trance-like state. It was not the color—which was the most dazzlingly beautiful molten gold, beyond anything I'd ever seen before—but the fierce, almost animal-like intensity of them. So heady they made my head swim. At that moment I would have willingly surrendered anything he wanted. Both my body and my mind felt as if they were under a spell, no longer in my control. As aroused and helpless as one of Count Dracula's victims!

For those few breathless seconds, we were no longer in the red-walled great dining room of the castle, but somewhere else, somewhere magical. There was no one else there except us. No Mr. Fellowes, no Ceba, or Misty.

Only me and the slowly roving, devouring, hypnotic eyes of a masked and powerful stranger poring over me. I felt overwhelmed. It seemed incredible that while I was blindfolded this tall and magnetic man had done sinfully delicious things to my naked body.

Then his lips moved. 'Good evening,' he drawled, his tone velvety and full of dark promise.

I shivered. His voice always stirred something inside me. Images of us coupling.

A strange desire to be taken in forbidden ways.

My lips parted as the breath rushed out of me. 'Hello.' My voice sounded high and small.

Mr. Fellowes left the room unobtrusively, and Guy came forward, pulled his chair out and sat. Ceba settled himself with a grunt by Guy's chair.

My eyes were drawn to his throat—darkly sensual against the white of his open shirt. He was wearing a black dinner jacket, but when he lifted his hands and put them on the table I noticed that he was wearing a black glove on his left hand. My gaze strayed to his right hand. It lay large and manly on the surface of the table. I remembered well the shape and the imprint it left on my body.

'I heard you at the piano today. You play very well,' he remarked.

Surprised by the compliment, I looked up and found him watching me intently. Unable to hold his gaze I dropped my eyes to his lips, and that was worse because I suddenly remembered when he had kissed me between my spread legs. Heat flooded into my cheeks. Oh God! What an obvious fool I was.

'Thank you,' I choked finally.

'Where did you learn to play?'

My hand fluttered nervously up to my throat. 'My mother taught all of us to play.'

'I thought your family were very poor.'

I dragged my gaze back to him. 'We were, but my mother was once the daughter of a very rich man. She lived in a fine house in Moscow and taught music and English. The piano was a relic of those times.'

'What happened then?'

'She married my father,' I said simply.

Mr. Fellowes returned carrying a tray. 'Cream of asparagus and mint,' he announced with a flourish and placed a bowl of thick green liquid with a cream swirl on its surface in front of me.

'Thank you,' I murmured, and watched him go around and place another bowl in front of Guy. Dipping the spoon into the smooth hot liquid I brought it to my lips. I had never tasted asparagus before. It was delicate and delicious.

I picked up the bread roll on my side plate, broke a small piece and buttered it.

'Tell me about your father.'

'My father was a hunter. He hunted elk, chinchillas, hares. Anything really. Once he shot a brown bear.' My voice was flat and dead.

'What kind of man was he?'

I put down my piece of bread and stared into my soup. 'What is it that you want to know about my father?'

'I want to know your history. I want to know how you came to be on the dark net waiting for a buyer.'

I bit my lip to stop it from trembling with the sudden hatred I felt for my father. 'After my mother married my father something happened. Something bad and they had to leave Moscow in a hurry. The only thing of value they took with them was my mother's piano. They moved to a tiny village wearing false names. And that is where we were all born, at the edge of a forest. Never meeting people, never going to school or on holidays, never having friends come around. And every year my father sold one of us because he believed it was his right to do so. After all, he had fed and sheltered and cared for us. Eventually, it became my turn.' I glanced up at him.

His eyes narrowed. 'You seem so removed from it all.'

I shrugged, remembering the sense of helplessness and frustration that I had felt all my life. 'There was never anything I could do. It was simply the way it was.' I swallowed nervously. My hands were so tightly clasped in my lap that the knuckles showed white. 'There is something you could do to help, though.' I looked up and met his mesmerizing eyes.

He picked up his glass and sipped the chilled amontillado from El Puerto de Santa Maria that Mr. Fellowes had brought up from the cobwebbed cellars. 'What?'

I held his gaze. 'I have a brother, a twin brother. I love him dearly. My father has sold eight of his children. He is the last. Please, could you please save him?' I stared at him with pleading eyes.

He became very still and looked at me over the rim of his glass. He did not say anything and his eyes were like the eyes of a wolf. Impossible to decipher anything. The seconds passed.

And I felt myself shrivel. I understood that I had asked too early. I should have waited. I was just a pleasant diversion. I was not meant to bring my problems to his table. I felt hot tears prick at the backs of my eyes. I hung my head in defeat and a strange thing happened. Ceba rose to his feet and leaving his master came and put his chin on my lap. The kindness that that fierce, aloof dog showed me was my undoing.

I covered my face with both my hands and sobbed.

Ceba began to paw at me with his great feet. He made small whining noises. I felt Mr. Fellowes come and stand next to me as if in support. When I had managed to compose myself, he held out a handkerchief for me. I took it and blew my nose. I was not defeated. I would find a way. I put my hand on Ceba's head and he looked at me with those timeless eyes of his. I thanked Mr. Fellowes. From the corner of my eye I could see that Guy had not moved at all. Mr. Fellowes removed the bowls and went out. I stared at the white linen placemat.

'I'm sorry. I know you have suffered,' Guy said suddenly, and his voice was strained and husky. And then he stood and left the dining room without having the main course that Mrs. Littlebell had slaved over: short-rib bourguignon. Ceba looked at me with mournful eyes one last time and followed his master out.

That night he did not send for me.

*****

I fell asleep and dreamed that I was young again and all of us were one big family living in the log house with the blue painted roof. My mother was still alive and Nikolai and I were snuggled up together in bed, sandwiched between our sisters, all our bodies warm and soft, while the winter night howled outside. We slept the sleep of the innocent, unaware of what awaited us in the future.

Chapter 16

When I woke up in the morning the sky was gray and it was raining. At breakfast Mr. Fellowes looked up from his toast and smiled his first real smile at me. It warmed his cold, long face up no end.

'Come and sit beside me,' he said, his pale face full of kindness. I shrugged at Misty, who raised her eyebrows in an enquiring and surprised way, and went to sit with Mr. Fellowes.

'What will you do today, lass?' he asked.

'I don't know. I guess I will explore. There is so much of the castle I haven't seen yet.'

'That's a good idea. You can start with the Countess Dufferin's room. I've heard that you are curious about her.' His eyes twinkled. 'She is the one who is supposed to be haunting this castle. Her room is very interesting. It has been preserved almost as she left it.'

'I'd love that,' I said. 'Do you know much about her, Mr. Fellowes?'

'Only what legend has, in that she took her own life and left instructions for her headstone and for her heart to be removed from her body and buried with the little girl, but her husband refused her request. He died soon after her. On his deathbed he was seen talking to thin air, saying, "I will do it. I promise I will do it. Please don't be angry with me.'"

After breakfast Mr. Fellowes took me to her room. He opened the door, switched on the lights for me and left. I closed the door and I felt her. Though hundreds of years had passed I felt her gentle touch. It was in the Chinoserie walls, with their depiction of a riverside scene and peacocks. Mr. Fellowes was right: it was hardly touched. I went and sat on her bed and shivered. The room was not heated and it was cold. The small hairs on the back of my neck stood. Suddenly I had the uncanny feeling that I was not alone. Someone or something was watching, but I was not afraid, because the spirit meant me no harm. In a funny sort of way I felt as if I belonged to the spirit.

As if in a daze I went to her beautiful writing desk. I opened a little drawer and as if my hand had been guided I turned my palm upwards and slid my fingers along the polished wood until they felt a little catch. I pressed it and the entire panel slid back to reveal two drawers.

A flash of excitement raced through me.

Many years ago, even hundreds of years, someone had hidden important things in those drawers. I carefully pinched the small knob and pulled one of the drawers open. There was a diary tied in a blue ribbon, a beautifully enameled green and blue box, and a faded, curling photograph of a young girl standing in a studio. She had fair hair and plump cheeks. Her eyes were bright and full of intelligence. She smiled carefully at the camera.

I put the photograph down and ran my fingers along the smooth, cool surface of the box. I took it out and carefully opened it and gasped. On a bed of velvet lay a five strand pearl choker with a cameo pendant. It was very old and very beautiful. I went to the mirror and held it around my neck. The owner was long dead. And I had found it. The clasp was diamond encrusted and still worked. I fixed it around my neck and held up my hair. I thought it suited me very well and I was truly pleased with it.

Touching it I went back to the diary. It was leather bound and well used. The edges were brown. I touched the old metal. It was only five inches by four—small—and yet I knew it held heartfelt secrets.

Was it right to read them?

And yet, she was long gone. I thought of her bent over her diary in the light of a single candle. She wouldn't care. Still I hesitated. It was locked, but the key was stuck to the back. Just a quick look. I pulled the key from its slot and opened the diary. A waft of lavender. Amazing. The scent had survived more than a hundred years. I thought of her pressing the flowers between the pages.

Beautiful handwriting declared the diary as belonging to Isabella Thorn Dufferin. I gasped. Oh my God, I was holding her diary. I touched the yellowing page and carefully held it between my fingers. I told myself I was not going to read the whole thing, I was only going to glimpse the past. Just quickly.

I turned the page.

It was like finding a secret garden. Captivating. Full of watercolor illustrations of flowers and leaves, a charming pig in coat and tails, and a man. A tall, broad-shouldered man with a stern face. Underneath the illustration she had written 'The Count of Dufferin'.

I told myself that I would just open it to the first page and read the start of the handwritten account of her life. Holding my breath I turned the page. The writing was small, and she had tried to cram as much as possible into the page. Around the words she had filled the spaces with delightful drawings and sketches.

I have come early to bed with a headache, but I can hardly sleep for excitement. There is no one else I can speak to but you, dear book of my wickedest hour—I smoked a cigar.

And just like that I was effortlessly transported into Isabella Thorn's lost world. I forgot the uncomfortable feeling of prying into the secret repository of another's thoughts. I took the diary to the window seat and curling up on the cushions began to read.

It was utterly engrossing. It started with the musings of an unusually spirited young girl. At this point there were sweet accounts of chance meetings during walks in parks with Mama and rebellion.

I long for things I ought not to prize... I often dine in haste and am too rebellious and unfeminine...

Following this was the willful intention to marry the womanizing Count Dufferin. Papa gave in and she won the day. There was a long account of her church wedding to the Count and the frank and sensual record of her marriage bed. I read it curiously and without blushing. She had worn the pearls for him.

My husband and I blush now to think of it, but he did not allow me to wear my undergarments when he took me.

'Leave only the pearls,' he instructed.

I had to take everything off, petticoats and corset, as he watched with the eyes of a hungry beast. When I tried to cover myself, he knocked my hands away with two precise practiced movements, using the tip of his cane.

He enjoyed my shame until I thought I would die with it. Then he hooked my neck with his cane and pulled me toward him. When he entered me it was hard, hot thrusts, and an animal-like growl of possessing and possession.

It was painful, but I would not have wanted different. It calmed my excitable nature. When it was finished, he made me do the unthinkable. Mama would have been so shocked but I did it and I enjoyed it. I wanted to please him. And please him I did.

For he rose again and had me again. Harder and even more painful.

'You are number two hundred and thirty,' he said.

I frowned. 'What do you mean?' I asked.

And he slapped me.

And while I was still in shock he used his fingers and played with me until I felt quite as if I might be ill. When I cried he told me to ride it. And the strangest thing happened to me, dear book. I blush to remember it, but it was a little as if I died and went to heaven. The pleasure was quite intolerable. Afterwards he kissed me. Now I understood. Now I understood.

It was as if I had written those words. I was not reading the diary of another but reading my own words. But the Count's passion didn't survive long. Soon there were no more illustrations of pigs or flowers. Only her deep dismay at her husband's infidelities. Hour after hour she gazed into the abyss of her love. *I am more lonely than ever, and more friendless than ever. My misery is a woman's misery*, she wrote. She quoted a line from William Allingham's sad poem, 'A Wife'. The wife sits over her diary and...

A tear—one tear—fell hot on the cover.

She became pregnant. Her pregnancy was poignant with her love for her unborn child and her woe at her husband's cold and uncaring treatment of her. After the birth of a girl the diary was suddenly lifted with drawings of posies and sunflowers. She knitted socks and a little coat. She dressed the child in them and took her into the garden. It was gentle exercise in daylight and pure air, surrounded by the sights, sounds, and smells of nature. She sat under the beech tree reading *Uncle Tom's Cabin*, but by now the Count had completely disentangled himself from her.

April 7th, Unusually miserable day.

She bore his rejection passively and made no stand against his mean and cruel ways. He flaunted his affairs openly. His mistresses made veiled comments at parties, and she retired to her lonely bed too much roused to sleep. She had been left with a dowry, which her husband had almost immediately appropriated.

Finally, she knew.

He had married her for money. She made new sketches of him. Unlike the earlier ones he seemed more narrow-faced and haughty.

Then her child died—she didn't say why or how—and her entries were filled with her unspeakable loss and grief. It was harrowing and disturbing to witness the way the diary had changed from breathless anticipation to this bleak bitterness. Face in both hands she knelt on the carpet and wept because, she wrote, *My heart is broken and can never be repaired.*

She was locked up in her room for being quite deranged, but her diary did not reveal her as the least bit mad. She was just too, too sad. The richly decorated diary became sparse.

Her collapse into despair was total.

My life is gone. The loss and pain are indescribable. Indescribable. And insufferable.

Her last line was disturbing.

I had a glass of sherry, which has given me a confused, smothering headache. I weary of myself and yet I cannot die. Prayer and silence shall alone be mine. My hand is as cold as marble.

And after that there were no more entries even though there were more pages.

Chapter 17

That night I lay in scented bathwater thinking of Isabella Thorn Dufferin. The water felt slippery with all the oils and powders I had poured into it. I thought of the Count, the way he had used his cane to remove her hands from her most intimate parts. Then I thought of Guy.

I got out of the bath and dressed in my green robe. And then I had a thought. I went to the box and took the pearl necklace out. I put it around my neck. I pulled my hair into a knot at the back of my head. Let it be the necklace that draws him. Let me see if I can hook Guy Hawke the way Isabella Thorn had hooked the Count. I looked foreign. My neck looked too long and delicate. The pearls had their own luster. I knew I looked different. I looked as if I belonged to a different time.

Misty came into my room.

'Wow,' she exclaimed. 'Where did you get that from?'

'I found it,' I told her.

'Where?'

'The dresser in the Countess's room has a secret drawer.'

'I see.' She paused. 'It's beautiful, but I don't think it's a good idea.'

I touched the necklace protectively. 'Why not?'

'What if he doesn't like it? My instructions are to take you naked.'

'I am naked. This is just a piece of jewelry.'

'All right. I suppose it doesn't matter.'

I smiled at her. 'I'll take the blame.'

'Damn right you will,' but she smiled to take the sting out of the words.

On the way to the room Misty looked at me sideways. 'Does this mean you are falling for him?'

I stood in shock. 'Why ever would you say that?'

'Why would you adorn yourself if not to attract someone you are attracted to?'

We reached the room silently. Misty blindfolded me and left. I heard the door shut and I took off my dressing gown and sat on the bed. Being blindfolded is a strange thing. It gives you a wolf's sense. What I would not have normally heard felt heavy in my ears. The sound of the fire roaring and the wind howling outside. Ren had said that there might be another storm tonight.

Even though the room was lovely and warm I shivered slightly.

Then, in the corridor, I heard the sound of his footsteps. It was strange how acute my hearing had become. Nervously, I waited for the steps to pause outside, for the door to open, and for him to stand inside the room. As always he closed the door and leaned against it, watching me. It seemed to me that he leaned against the door watching me longer than usual.

He strode toward me and I felt not lust or admiration, but anger coming off in waves from his body. His fingers brushed my throat roughly and the necklace chain was ripped from me. In a daze I heard the pearls land on the floor and roll away in every which direction.

He leaned close to my ear. His voice was harsh. 'Don't adorn yourself for me,' he said, and slowly swiped a pearl along my bottom lip.

'Why?' I whispered, hurt and confused. The pearl slipped and made a tapping sound on my teeth.

'Because,' he said very softly, 'you are already too unendurably beautiful.'

My heart tripped in my chest.

'And I don't want you to play any little games with me either.' His voice was laced with sensual menace.

I frowned. 'I wasn't playing games.'

He caught my earlobe in his teeth. 'No?'

So quickly had his scent become familiar. 'No.'

'And another thing. Don't put your hair up again while you are with me. I don't like it.'

I drew a sharp breath. He yanked the pin holding my hair in its knot. It fell heavily onto my shoulders.

I licked my lips. It was insane how seductive was the call of desire, how much I wanted him to touch me, kiss me, fuck me.

He rubbed his palms lightly on my nipples. 'So sweet and so innocent. Little Lena: never been with anyone.'

Zara flashed into my mind. And the things she did to me.

His hand stilled. There was something dark and predatory about his stillness, like an animal that crouches before it lunges. 'You *have* been with someone?' His voice was silky, but oh! So alert.

My lower lip trembled. 'The woman... The woman who kept me in the cage. She did things to me and I to her.'

He expelled his breath in a furious hiss. His fingers pinched my nipples.

I bit my lip. 'I had to. To survive.'

His hands relaxed suddenly. 'Of course,' he said softly, and ran his palm lightly on the tips of my breasts again. The touch was so delicate that I shuddered. Gooseflesh scattered on my skin. But some violence lurked behind the gentle caress.

'Have you never done something shameful to survive?' I asked defiantly.

'Yes.' His voice was unemotional and cold.

I was shocked. I had not really expected him to answer me. 'What?' I whispered.

'I bought you.'

'What do you mean?' I asked gazing into the darkness of the blindfold. There was nothing there but darkness and the unknown. I could feel him frowning, thinking... Furious.

'The woman who kept you in the cage... Did she hurt you?'

I thought of Zara. Of the sickening smell of her, of the skin that was like that of rotting apple or the things she had made me do for a *tomato*. I thought of how she had degraded me and humiliated me, taken my clothes, turned me into an animal. At that moment I rose above my own pain and realized that it was a terrible way to go through life. I knew I didn't hate her. She was profoundly sad and lonely. I pitied her. I thought of her in her farmhouse and I wondered who would be in the cage now.

'No,' I said softly. 'She did not hurt me. She used me because she was lonely. The same way you do.'

His hand left my body. 'She took what did not belong to her. I take what is mine,' he snarled. 'And if you were not such a fucking child you would know that.' He stood suddenly over me. I knew he was looking at me with those irresistibly magnetic eyes of his.

'I'm not a child,' I said.

He sighed. The sound came from deep within him. 'Promises are meant to be kept,' he said, but he was not talking to me. He was talking to himself.

'What promises?' I asked, but he didn't want to tell me. They were his secrets. Would the day ever come when he would trust me enough to bring me into his world?

'Open your legs,' he ordered.

I did and the sex was undeniably good. As it always was. Then he got up and left. That night I found it hard to sleep. I kept remembering Nikolai's face when I said goodbye to him. I had to find a way to keep my promise to him.

Chapter 18

'**S**ome boxes arrived for you,' Misty said, when I got back for lunch.

'For me?' I asked, surprised.

'Yeah, dresses I think Guy ordered them from London. You are to choose one and wear it tonight. You are having dinner with him.'

I stared at her. 'He bought me dresses?'

'Well, come look,' Misty encouraged.

We opened the boxes together. There were five dresses. A long white one with thin spaghetti straps, a green mini dress with round cut-outs at the hem and waist, a slinky oyster-colored knee-length dress, a long black dress with a daringly cut low back and high slits along the side, and a pretty red dress with a little box jacket. There were shoes to match with every dress.

Misty stroked the dresses longingly. 'How beautiful. Each one of these must have cost what I make in a whole year.'

I was shocked. 'Really?'

'Absolutely. This one with the metal cut-outs is the latest Versace design. I saw it in a fashion video.'

I took the green dress and held it up against her body. 'It looks really well with your auburn hair.'

She looked at me wistfully. 'Yeah, green is my color.'

'Why don't you have it?'

'What?'

I grinned at her. 'It suits you, so why not?'

She looked incredulous. 'You're *giving* this dress to *me*?'

'That's what it looks like.'

She laughed. 'Are you sure about this?'

'Yes.' I laughed. It felt good to be able to make someone happy.

'Oh my God! I can't believe I am now the owner of a genuine Versace! Thank you, Lena. Thank you. It's so generous of you.'

I touched her. 'No, thank you. You've always been so kind to me.'

She looked embarrassed. 'Which one will you wear tonight?'

I didn't have to look at the selection. 'The black one. I've never worn black in my life.'

'Goodness! Really?'

I nodded. 'Yeah. All I ever had was hand-me-downs.'

'Well, the black one is very beautiful. With your blonde hair it will look stunning.'

'Do you have some lipstick that I can borrow?'

She hugged her green dress close to her chest and grinned happily. 'Lipstick? Yes, I have lipstick you can have.'

'Do you have red lipstick?'

She frowned. 'Yes, but a softer color might be better for you since you have a complexion like double cream.'

I smiled. 'No, today I want to wear red.'

'Red it is.'

*****

That evening I poured some of the scented oils I found in the bathroom cabinet into the bath and soaked in the deliciously silky water until it got cold. Then I quickly washed my hair and climbed out. I switched on that amazing invention called the hair dryer and soon my hair was lying in soft waves down my back. Then, wearing no underwear, I slipped into the black dress. Misty had brought the lipstick up for me earlier and I very carefully, taking my time, colored my lips. The transformation was shocking. I marveled at it. My lips looked so big and full and out of proportion to the rest of my face. My mouth seemed to jump out of my face. I wondered if Misty had been right with her advice of keeping it soft. I smiled at myself. No, I didn't want to be soft and sweet, I wanted to look daring and sexy.

I chose the red shoes in favor of the black. They were very high, but I found that I had no trouble walking in them. While going down the stairs, though, I did have to clutch at the banister until the last step.

When I went into the dining room I was surprised to see the table set with vases of blood red roses and lighted candelabras. Mr. Fellowes turned toward me, and his eyebrows shot into his receding hairline.

'Do I look all right?' I asked nervously.

'You're a sight for sore eyes, lass,' he said warmly.

'Is the red lipstick too red?'

'No. It's perfect.'

'I hope Guy thinks so.'

'He'd be bonkers not to.'

I laughed, my laughter dying in my throat at the sound of footsteps outside the door. I turned toward the door and Guy was standing there. He stood motionless. We stared at each other. Something leapt in his eyes and then it was gone so quickly I could not be sure I had really seen it. I smiled shakily. His sensual lips twitched. Candlelight reflected on his mask.

'Thank you for the dress and the shoes.'

He walked into the room and came to stand a foot away. He reached out a hand and touched my lips. 'Lipstick,' he said wonderingly.

'Misty lent—'

He stilled my words by putting his finger across my lips. 'You look beautiful.'

The longer he stared at me, the more my skin prickled and small vibrations of heat rippled the surface of my body and pooled at my center. I swallowed hard and he put his hand on the small of my back and guided me to my seat. I sat then watched him take his with easy grace. He was wearing a gray silk shirt, a white dinner jacket and black trousers. He looked very confident and sophisticated. Mr. Fellowes poured wine into my glass and then his. He lifted his glass. 'To lipstick.'

I lifted mine. 'To lipstick.'

We drank. For some strange reason I felt nervous. I put my glass down. Mr. Fellowes had left the room to bring out the first course.

'Misty says that you told her you think you've seen a ghost.'

'Mmm.'

'What sort of a ghost?' he asked curiously.

'A lady. I can never see her face.'

'Does she frighten you?'

'No, it feels as if I belong to her... A little.'

'What does she do when she appears?'

'She cries for her child.'

He stiffened; his eyes became suddenly bleak and out of all proportion to what we were talking about.

I rushed into speech. 'Mr. Fellowes told me that it might be the Countess Isabella. Her baby died, and even though she left instructions that her heart must be cut out and buried with her child, her husband did not do it so she roams restlessly.'

He seemed to control himself. 'That sounds a bit like a Gothic myth.'

'No, it's on her gravestone. She requested it. We should dig up the baby's bones and bury it with hers.'

He looked at me as if I was mad. '*I* will not be doing any such thing.'

'It's what she wants,' I insisted.

Mr. Fellowes came in with our first course. He put down a plate of food too beautiful to eat, and said, 'Langoustine tails with Parmesan gnocchi and truffle emulsion.'

'Bon appétit,' said Guy.

'Bon appétit,' I replied and we ate and drank and afterwards ate jasmine tea-smoked venison, pickled blueberries and black garlic.

When the meal was over Mr. Fellowes bade us goodnight and left, closing the door behind him.

Guy stood and came over, took my hand and pulled me upright. Instantly, the air around us changed. I looked into his eyes. Desire, hot and urgent, blazed in them.

He pulled the bodice of my dress down to my waist exposing my naked breasts to his gaze, and lifting me by the waist put me on the table. Gently, he lowered me onto the table until I was lying on it with my legs hanging down.

Not taking his eyes off me he fetched the bottle of champagne from the ice bucket and after peeling the gold foil, upended the bottle on me. Chilled liquid foam splashed onto my breasts and chest.

I gasped, my muscles clenching and contracting against the cold, and he bent his head and licked and slurped at the cool bubbles on my skin. His mouth and tongue were so hot and exciting against my freezing skin, my thighs became wet with my arousal.

He took the tip of my breast between his teeth and I trembled from head to toe with anticipation and excitement. He bit down to an almost painful degree and tugged upwards pulling me along until I was arched and resting precariously on my elbows. His teeth released my aching nipple. The breath I had been holding escaped in a moan.

'I like it when you moan.'

I licked my lips slowly.

'Show me,' he demanded huskily.

I furled my fingers on the material of my dress at thigh level and slowly, inch by inch, pulled it up and over my hips. His eyes were riveted on my moving hemline. At the sight of my bare sex his eyes rushed up to meet mine.

'Excellent,' he said.

I said nothing.

'What comes next...?'

I raised both legs up, rested my shoes on his chest, and let my legs drop open.

He laughed. 'You learn fast,' he said, staring greedily at my open, swollen pussy.

Cool air drifted over my naked sex.

'Beautiful,' he said softly and brought his gaze back to mine. His eyes were like twin flames. Glowing and golden. They were dazzlingly glorious. Something about exposing myself to him ratcheted up my arousal another notch, and my sex started to throb.

His fingertips landed on my inner thighs. They moved up lightly. Where they touched my skin sizzled. He stopped just before he reached my pulsating core.

'What do you want, little seagull?'

I shook my head, unable to say a word.

'Nothing to say?'

I shook my head.

'Do you know what I want?'

I shook my head.

'I want to hold you wide open and eat you for hours. Then I want to make you come in my mouth and drink your juices, and afterwards I want to fuck you until you sob.'

I bit my lips.

'Too dirty for you?'

I shook my head.

'That's what I thought too.'

And he bent his head and licked and sucked my pussy until I burst open and climaxed in his mouth and as he had promised he licked it all up and started again with a real and rabid hunger until I was flushed and drunk with sensations and thought my body could not bear another second of his tongue.

'Please,' I begged, my voice a gentle breeze.

His eyelids closed a little so they hooded his eyes. Then his fingers tightened on my thighs and his strong hands pulled me to the very edge of the table. 'You're so fucking sexy,' he growled and sank his thick, hard cock in me, and fucked me again and again until I sobbed with release.

I lay on the table, exhausted, my mind foggy, my dress bunched around my waist, my hair a mess, my breasts exposed, my legs splayed and dripping with his seed, and watched with glazed eyes as he pulled up his trousers, zipped them and did up his belt. I wondered what I must have looked like. Perhaps what I was: a sexual slave who had just been thoroughly used by her master.

He looked at my open legs and I saw desire flare up, as intense as it had been at the beginning of the night. I waited until his eyes met mine.

'It's all right if you don't want to help my brother, but will you at least allow Misty to post the letters I write to him?'

I saw the expression in his eyes change. I blinked and it was gone. His eyes shuttered and became blank. He moved with deadly grace, quickly away from me. At the door he turned, not fully. 'Give the envelope to me tomorrow.'

He was gone before I could thank him.

Chapter 19

Hawke

I walked up the steep curving steps of the tower to the very top. I opened the door and stood for a moment at the doorway looking in. It was a bare room with just a narrow bed, a wooden table and a chair, but it was a place that had soothed me in the past. When I first moved into this castle I spent most of my days here. Alone and drunk.

Those were the dark days.

After the accident when the world outside became too much to take, I would sit at the table and drink until I no longer felt any pain, and then I would lie on that uncomfortable bed with its broken springs, close my eyes, and completely empty my mind of everything, but sailing on the wide open ocean. All my concentration would be on the direction of the wind in my sails, keeping the boat upright, and flying through miles of the waves.

Never would there be anyone but me. I never needed anyone while I was at sea, only the heat of the midday sun beating down on my skin. All my pains, my worries, my fears, and my terrible, terrible fury would simply seep away for a few hours. It would be just me on a little boat completely free and totally connected with the elements.

But those dark days passed, and I hardly ever needed to come here anymore.

I closed the door and went to the table. There were only two items on it. A bottle of bourbon and a glass. I sat at the table and poured myself a drink. I knocked it back and welcomed the burn. I poured another drink. Some alcohol spilled on the table. I rubbed my finger in it absent-mindedly. There was pain today. A new kind of pain. A fresh pain.

I touched my face: it felt vile. The skin was thick and hard, but no sensation at all—every nerve ending had been fried. I could still clearly remember how my skin had curled like the pages of a burning book. For the longest time I didn't even want to see what my face looked like, or feel it. The transformation was so drastic. I had thought that I would never again care what I looked like. But now my appearance mattered again. And it was because of her.

The more I pushed her away, the more entangled I became. I was drawn to her like I had never been to anyone or anything. I longed to crawl into her pure, childlike soul and rest a while, but I knew that doing that would only destroy me. Her face shimmered in my mind.

I quickly knocked back a large shot and followed that with another. I didn't want to think about her. It was all a fucking mess.

Half a bottle later, I lay on the bed, closed my eyes and heard again the furious flapping of the sail boat, the sound of the water hitting the hull. The fresh scent of the ocean and the total freedom of being at sea. I looked into the sky and I saw a seagull. It circled me and I opened my eyes.

Never before had that happened. I was always alone. I was always totally in control. There was never more than me and the elements. And now she had corrupted my only safe haven.

Chapter 20

Lena

The next morning I woke up early, sat at the writing desk and wrote to Nikolai. The letter was five pages long. I knew my father would never allow him to write back, but that didn't matter, as long he knew I had not forgotten my promise. I sealed it in an envelope and went down for breakfast.

At the bottom of the stairs I met Ceba coming in from the kitchens. He wagged his great big tail, gave my hand a sniff and a lick, and looked at me with begging eyes.

'I'll have something for you later,' I promised, stroking his head. I looked up and Misty was staring at me.

'You've made friends with him,' she said, her tone laced with disbelief.

'Yeah, when we were small my brother and I made friends with a wolf cub.' I grinned. 'So I'm good with big, wild animals.'

'Wow! Your life sounds like it must have been a fantastic adventure,' she said brightly.

She had no idea. 'It wasn't,' I said quietly. And my tone told her I didn't want to talk about my past.

We walked into the breakfast room together.

'Will you see Guy this morning?' I asked her.

'Yeah, I'm just about to go to his study and give him a report.'

A report. I wondered what sort of report she was going to give him, but she had categorically told me that she wasn't going to reveal any information about Guy to me.

'Can you give this letter to him to post? I really want it to go out as soon as possible.'

She took the letter and looked at it. 'Russia?'

'Yes, it is for my brother.'

'I see. All right. I'll give it to him this morning. It can go out with all the lunchtime mail.'

'Thank you.' I smiled brightly at her. I was so happy. I was making progress. I had a plan. If I could find a way of making a bit of money, by selling some of my clothes or doing some kind of work, I could start to save up and in this way get Nikolai out of Russia. I had no idea how I was going to arrange for his passport or visa or his plane ticket, but I just knew that step by step I would somehow be reunited with my brother.

*****

It began to rain that afternoon and I decided to explore the east wing of the castle. Misty told me that that was where the ballroom was. The double doors creaked open and its empty darkness intrigued me and drew me in. I could see the light switches, but I did not use them. Instead I walked into the echoing dim and tried to imagine what this place must have been like during the time of Isabella.

The patter of my footsteps on the antique flagstones was the only sound in the strange stillness. As if dancing to music I lifted my hands as if they were resting on a man's shoulders and, holding onto an imaginary hand, I began to twirl around.

I heard a sound and as I whirled around to face it I was grabbed from behind. I screamed. A gloved hand covered my mouth. How quickly that hand had become familiar to me. I leaned back with relief against the hard chest, no longer afraid.

It must have only been seconds but it seemed like forever that we stared at each other in perfect silence. His eyes seemed so dark, and the thickly fringed black lashes even more pronounced. Then I blinked and the moment was broken.

'Would you do me the honor of this first dance?'

'Yes.'

He slid his arm around my waist and pulled me closer so my body was molded to the hard muscles. I am five feet nine inches tall, but even so he towered over me, making me feel small and defenseless. He began to move and take me along with him. With total trust I submitted to his lead. At first our movements were slow and careful as our bodies learned to match the other, but soon we were making large circles and he was spinning me so fast I felt a little dizzy. I looked into his eyes and felt totally safe; it felt as if nothing could ever hurt me here. I became a part of him, I felt every breath he took, I mirrored exactly every move he made.

'Ah, Lena,' he whispered in my ear.

His voice made me tremble with anticipation. He stopped moving and started to kiss my throat. A moan escaped my mouth and my breath rattled unsteadily through my teeth. I wanted him. I wanted him like I had never wanted another human being. With every inch of my being I ached for him.

'Tell me what you want?' I whispered.

'I want you to get on your knees and milk me.'

I got on my knees and finding the zipper of his trousers pulled it down. He was rock hard. I kissed the hard, tight flesh above the band of his underwear. The warmth of his skin melted into me and sent delicious tingles down my spine. I remembered how I had felt when he had kissed me between my legs and I took him out of his boxers and kissed him gently and sweetly on the tip of his hard length.

He drew a sharp breath.

Immediately, I slid the long length of him into my open mouth and as I bobbed on him,

I sucked hard. So hard my cheeks hollowed. He groaned and stroked my hair, while his gloved hand gripped my shoulder. I looked up at him and he was avidly watching the length of him disappearing in and out of my greedy, noisy mouth.

I worked on him, slowly increasing my pace until his cock became so big in my mouth that I knew from experience that he was nearly there. My mouth flew faster and faster along his shaft. Then he began to thrust his hips, the way he did when he was fucking me. I felt his shaft go so deep into my throat that I began to gag. He held my head and continued, until he came with hot spurts of thick salty cream. I swallowed it all, and still did not remove his semi-hard cock from inside my mouth for a few seconds more.

'I'd like to fall asleep with my cock inside your mouth,' he said.

So I began to suck his cock very gently. It quivered appreciatively in my mouth so I gave it more. To my delight it hardened a little more. Of course that made me suck it even harder and it responded. I must have stayed on my knees making it grow in my mouth for at least ten minutes. But it worked. He pulled out of my mouth fully erect. He hauled me up and took me to a wall

'Put your hands out.'

I put my hands out against the wall and felt his hands come around my body and undo the top button on my jeans, the zip, and then my jeans and my scrap of underwear were sliding down. He hunkered down and picked up my foot and looped the material off.

Then he widened my stance and, pulling my hips toward him, drove his cock into me and pounded away forcefully until I lost the ability to think. I was just an animal being fucked by another animal. He roared, close to my ear, a primal sound that came from deep within and echoed in the vast, empty room.

At that moment my flesh shook and jerked as a burst of sensation exploded between my legs, and my climax began. From deep within it came. And on and on it went. I would have fallen. He had to hold me close to his body. I leaned against his hard body and came back slowly.

'We came in unison,' he observed quietly.

'Yes, it was lovely.'

I didn't want to move. I wanted us to remain close like that forever. But very gently he turned me around and, crouching, he fitted my leg into my knickers and pulled them up. He dressed me like a child and kissed me on the top of my head.

'I love these tendrils of wet hair that cling to your face,' he whispered.

I gently blew into his eye.

Immediately I felt his muscles tighten. 'What are you doing?'

'When I was a little girl, at night my mother used to ask me, "How did Joseph's scent come to Jacob?" And even though I knew the answer I would shake my head so she could tell me again. "The same way your scent will come to me. In the wind," she used to say and blow into my eye. "Besides a little wind cleans the eye," she used to joke.'

'You loved your mother very much, didn't you?'

'Yes,' I said instantly.

'You never talk about your father.'

'I hate him.'

'Did he beat you?'

'Never. He never hit any of his children. It wasn't necessary. We obeyed him in all things. We learned from very young that he was a mad man. He loved my mother and screamed when she died, and yet he was willing to boil her hand while her children watched in horror.'

'What?'

'Yes, he did that to punish me.'

'You've had a rotten life, haven't you?'

'Yes.'

'Are you—? Never mind. I'll see you at dinner,' he said, breaking our fragile closeness and turning to go.

I caught his hand. 'Am I what, Guy?'

'Nothing,' he lied.

I watched his tall, broad figure walk away from me and felt sad. He seemed so alone. So unreachable. I knew there was so much more I wanted from him. So much I wanted to know about him.

'Guy,' I called. My voice echoed in the vast room.

He stopped and turned his thickly muscled chest toward me. In the half-light I met his gaze with soft, imploring eyes. There was so much I wanted to say, but at that moment I couldn't think of a thing.

'Switch on the lights on your way out, please.'

He nodded and when he reached the doorway, flicked on the switch, and left without looking back.

Up above, the giant chandeliers, hanging like glory-clouds from the lofty ceilings, came on. I gazed up in wonder and imagined guests in grand clothes waltzing under these dazzling clouds of lights. Then the velvet curtains of deepest plum were not dappled with mildew, and the gray stone walls did not cry out with the loneliness of their owner.

Chapter 21

The weeks passed strangely. The days were spent wandering aimlessly around the cold, damp castle or exploring the grounds waiting for the hot nights. Waiting for Guy to consume me with his passion. I found an old cassette player in the library and racks of music cassettes from the sixties, seventies and eighties. When I asked Misty about it she said it belonged to nobody, and since nobody wanted it, I could have it.

Overjoyed, I brought it up to my room. The sound was a bit scratchy and sometimes the reels got caught and chewed inside the machine, and I would have to carefully remove the tape from the machine, insert my finger into the middle of the spools and slowly feed them back in, but I loved my cassette player. I spent hours when the weather was bad lying on my bed alone listening to music.

That day Guy had gone off to London in the helicopter and would not be back until the next. I spent the morning wandering about the castle and ended up outside his study. I had never been in it. And I had never been forbidden to go into it. I tried the door and to my surprise it opened.

It was large and dimly lit but warmer than the corridor. The walls were totally bare and painted white. There was a daybed with green and blue cushions on it and there was a low cabinet with bottles of alcohol on it. Other than that there was only a steel cabinet, and a very large desk with a black leather swivel chair behind it. The surface of the table was covered in green leather. There was nothing on it but a fountain pen. I went and sat on the chair. It was very comfortable and so big I could curl up in it. So, this was where Guy did whatever it was that he did.

My eyes were drawn to one of the drawers. It was slightly ajar. As if Guy had closed it that morning in a hurry and had not quite finished the job. I knew I shouldn't be rifling through his drawers, but that half an inch gap was like a magnet. Without really thinking of the consequences of my actions I put my index finger in it and pulled it open. And my mouth dropped open with shock.

The envelope addressed to Nikolai in my own handwriting was in it.

For a second I did not move. I could not believe what I was seeing. Then I picked it up and my other letters were underneath it. All five. He had not sent a single one of my letters. I took them in my hands, looked at the backs. They were unopened, untampered with.

Just not sent.

I felt anger like a ball of boiling anger erupting in my belly. My jaw clenched. Why? Why didn't he send my letters? Why did he pretend? Why did he lie to me? There was a noise outside in the corridor. I hastily put the letters back in the drawer and closed it. I felt disorientated and confused. Footsteps neared the door and Misty walked through it.

'Oh,' she said, surprised.

'Hi,' I said quietly.

'What are you doing here?'

'Nothing,' I said and shot upright.

'Are you all right?'

I took a deep breath. 'Yes. Do you know when Guy is coming back?'

'Tomorrow. Probably lunchtime.'

'OK. Thanks.'

She looked at me strangely, but I walked past her, almost brushing her. I was shaking with anger. I felt her turn to look at me. I did not turn back. I walked down the corridor in a confused daze. Why? Why would he do such a thing? What harm could it do for me to write to Nikolai?

Once in my room I was unable to settle. I paced it like a caged animal. I took my mother's lace from the drawer and held it against my cheek, but there was no comfort to be gained.

He had cheated me.

The weather outside was horrible, cold and blustery, but in the end I could bear the thick walls, the horrible thoughts in my head no more. I slipped into my coat and ran out of the great wooden doors. There was no Ceba to follow me that day. He had gone with Guy to have his teeth cleaned at a specialist vet in London.

It was true that I was so miserable and angry I wanted to be alone and away from everybody, but I wanted Ceba. He was not human and could be trusted. I desperately wished he was around. He was the first one to show me real love. He laid his chin on my lap and tried to comfort me that first night at dinner with Guy. If he had been here he would surely have followed me. I began to walk blindly away from the castle.

At the end of the archway I looked at the hill.

It looked wild and forbidding, but I had always loved the thought of high, wild places, and at that moment I knew that to climb it would be a good release for my anger and frustration and confusion. I gazed up at the horizontal rock jutting out from the peak of the hill. At that moment it called to me.

I walked quickly to its edge and began to climb it. Where the slope was not steep I made fast progress over the tussocky grass. Finally, I reached a ledge where the climbing had become decidedly harder. Breathing hard, I stopped climbing and turned my face up to the heavens. Instead of feeling better I felt even more angry and hurt. It seemed as if everything I did always took me nowhere.

There was no one I could trust or who would ever help me. I had really believed him. I thought he cared some, just a little bit. Just enough to post a letter for me.

But he didn't.

Tears prickled the backs of my eyes, but I didn't let them fall. The weather was changing. A wind was picking up and it whipped its cold breath across my cheek. Like a warning. But I gritted my teeth and ignored it. A fresh surge of adrenalin pumped into my blood. I tightened my hold and inched forward. I would get to the top of that rock or die trying. Fury made me reckless.

More by feel and instinct I found purchase for my hands and feet. The muscles of my arms and thighs were beginning to seriously ache. I looked down and saw the tremendous drop underneath and for a second actually felt the lure of it. To end it all. Never to have to cry and pine for my brother or to contemplate Guy's betrayal.

But the moment passed as quickly as it had come.

I would not give up. I would never betray my brother. I made a promise and I intended to keep it. Somehow I would find a way to help him. As for my hurt heart, it would heal. And I would *never* again trust Guy.

Another blast of blustery freezing wind slammed into me, making me almost lose my balance. Without my noticing it the ridge had become so narrow that I was hugging the rock surface to carry on climbing. And for the first time I felt fear. I could fall to my death from up here. I knew I should begin the trek back down.

I put a foot back but instead of the hard, firm surface of the rock I was putting my weight on sticky red sandstone mud, which disintegrated under me. My foot slipped and for a second I was hanging in the air, perfectly balanced, and then that second was gone and I was falling, twigs scraping my face and hands, and entangling themselves in my hair.

The wind was rushing into my neck and body. I tumbled painfully against rocks, arms flailing, like a drowning woman, clutching wildly at anything and missing. I could not even open my voice to scream—fear paralyzed my body. I hurtled toward the bottom at a speed that would most likely kill me.

My end seemed inevitable.

But even as that thought flashed into my head my grasping hands caught an overhanging branch. A tree that was growing on a narrow ledge. I grabbed it with both hands and pulled myself up to the ledge and lay the only way I could, on my side and hanging onto the branch.

Every inch of me hurt.

Gingerly, I moved my leg and shooting pain stabbed through my ankle. It was so strong it snatched the breath from my body. I cursed when flakes of snow started falling softly from the darkening sky. I had lost my cap during my fall and already the hair at my temples was plastered wetly against my head. Soon my clothes would be soaking wet too. My face was full of scratches and my limbs felt stiff.

My exertions had kept me warm so far, but now the frigid air crept around me. I knew the chill would first make a soft blanket and then it would seep into my skin, chilling my blood and like a hungry rat gnawing its way into the very marrow of my bones, even as the bare rock underneath me stole my heat. Would Misty know to send out a search party or would she just assume I was going to raid the fridge later? Who would she send, anyway? I could die overnight on this rocky ledge.

Damn you, Guy. I believed you. How stupid and naïve I had been. Now I knew without any doubt at all. I was just a body to him, a body he had bought to be used. A nothing. My personal tragedy meant nothing to him. He was worse than my father. At least my father never lied to us.

At that moment I hated Guy with a passion.

Suddenly the raw grief at the unfairness of my life brought tears pouring down my cheeks. Sorrow for Nikolai bubbled up from deep within. He was waiting for me. The tears that I had denied earlier filled my eyes. I sobbed so hard my chest hurt. I cried for a long time, but eventually I was all done in, emotionally, mentally, and physically. I was too exhausted and spent to do anything but hold on. I looked at my hands—they were frozen around the tree branch, and they were strangely blue-gray.

I started to feel a little floaty and weird. It was not a bad feeling. My mind felt distant and disconnected from my body. There were no more sensations coming from my body, not cold, or pain, or fear. I could still vaguely feel the hard rock beneath me, the sound of the angry wind buffeting the rocks, but it was all so far away and not really happening to me.

I knew instinctively that I shouldn't give in to this odd sensation of slipping away, but I could not fight it. I thought of Guy and all the anger was gone, only sadness remained. I wanted to hold onto him, really I did, but the pull of sleep was stronger. He had betrayed me anyway. He did not care. He had never cared. There was no point holding on. I stopped fighting to remain conscious.

I closed my eyes and my mind began to float in a void, almost a lake of nothingness. This must be death, I thought. In the end, my demise would be a merciful thing, after all.

But the strangest thing happened then. A woman was walking toward me. It was not Isabella. I had never seen her before in my life. She was tall with an unusual face: pretty green eyes, honey-brown hair, and a square jaw with a little pointed chin, which made her seem catlike, and very determined. 'Just hold on,' she said. Her voice was like glass tinkling.

'I'm only waiting for her, and then I'll be gone.'

There seemed to be some terrible sadness about her.

My eyes jolted open. There was no one there, but the cold, the snow, the wind, the dark, and the pain. She was not real. I realized I had begun to hallucinate. Her voice and image had been generated inside my head. I began to shiver uncontrollably. My teeth were chattering so hard that even clenching them did not help. Then I heard rocks skittering. Voices calling. A black shadow with glowing eyes loomed from the ledge above.

Ceba. He barked. Small pebbles came sliding down the rock face and hit me.

More voices. Guy. Ren.

Then Guy's masked face was peering down at me. His eyes were holes of panic and fear and seemed so dark that they reminded me of bat wings, shiny black skin stretched tight over bone. They hoisted me up to the wider ledge. Ceba's warm, wet tongue on my face was nice.

'You came,' I muttered drowsily out of numb lips, and passed out.

When I regained consciousness, Guy was carrying me. My cold face was in contact with the skin of his neck. I tried to cling to his warmth, to the safety of his hard muscles, but my hands as if outside my control and coordination fell about clumsily.

'I've got you,' he said into my hair, and I drifted out again.

When I came to my ankle was throbbing like crazy, but I was in a deliciously warm cocoon, tucked up under blankets. Even my neck and head were covered. My hands seemed to be bandaged. I couldn't remember much of our journey back. I kept gaining and losing consciousness.

Guy was sitting on a chair close to my head. He looked strained and exhausted and lost in his own deep thoughts. I wriggled my fingers in their bandages. The small movement made his hypnotic eyes swivel down to me. They burned into me, alert and watchful... And sad. Probably an after effect of worrying that his sex doll might have died up on the ledge and he would have had to get a new one.

My fury returned, now that I no longer thought I was dying.

'You're safe now,' he said. 'The doctor is coming, but I don't think you have any broken bones. Just cuts and bruises and a sprained ankle. Would you like something to drink?'

I nodded and he opened a Thermos flask and poured something into a mug then, dropping a straw in it, held it close to my lips. I sipped at it, the sweet, hot tea running down my parched tongue. I lay my head back slowly. Every muscle in my body hurt and I felt bone-deep weary, but my mind was wide awake and alive with questions.

'What were you doing? You could have died up there.' There was barely leashed fury in his voice.

'Why didn't you post my letters?' I whispered, and without even being conscious of it, tears started running down my temples.

His eyes narrowed, and I sensed the palpable tension in his body. 'Were you running away?'

'No, they will hurt Nikolai if I do.'

Something flashed in his eyes. He became unnaturally motionless. He didn't even seem to be breathing.

'What is it? What's wrong?' I asked, frightened by his reaction.

'Nothing,' he said and dropped his gaze so I would not see the expression in it.

'So why didn't you post my letters?' I asked again.

'I'm sorry I didn't.' His voice was strained.

I frowned, genuinely confused. 'You're sorry?'

'You need to rest.'

'Will I never be allowed to leave this castle?'

'I can't let you go, Lena,' he whispered.

And I became furious. 'Even the woman who caged me and forced me to submit to her sexual demands did not make me suffer indefinitely.'

I heard the chair being pushed back. I heard the muffled sound of his shoes on the shabby carpet. His breath fanned my neck, heat from his body radiating out. And he whispered in my ear, 'I have never pretended to be better than her.'

My voice was less than a whisper. 'Please let me go.'

'I can't,' he muttered, and then his heat moved away. I heard the soft footfalls of his step. I heard his weight land on the chair. I felt empty inside. Was this to be my life? Would I never leave here? Would I remain his toy forever? And what of Nikolai if I couldn't even write to him?

'Don't you understand I can never be happy here...without Nikolai. He is a part of me.'

He uttered a deep-throated growl like an animal that is in terrible pain and wants to ward off anyone approaching, and raised his hand as if he was about to touch my face, then let it fall. The gesture was one of defeat.

'A year. You may leave in a year.' The words had been torn from him.

Would Nikolai be able to wait for a whole year? No, he would not. I made a small sound.

'What is it?' he asked.

'My brother... He is suffering in his nest of thorns. My father is abusing him. My letter will be his only joy. Will you at least let me write to him?'

'You can write to your brother and give your letters to Misty to post. Tell her to claim the postage costs from petty cash.'

I nodded. Somehow it didn't seem like a victory.

'Now rest.'

A year. I closed my eyes and sleep came almost immediately. While I was sleeping I had the impression that a hand came to hold mine. It was familiar and strong and it was full of love. I clung to it, but in the morning there was no sign of it.

Chapter 22

In two days I was fine again. I sat up in bed and my fingers were stiff and blistered but I wrote a long letter to Nikolai and gave it to Misty.

'I'll get a receipt for you,' she said.

'Oh yes, please,' I said, relieved that finally there would be proof that my letter had been sent.

That afternoon I had a receipt. The address of the post office had been cut out of the receipt. It seemed that I was not to know where I was.

My ankle was still swollen, but Misty had brought me crutches and I could hobble around the castle. Ceba slept in my room a lot. Guy came to see me sometimes two or three times a day, but there was a new tension between us. Whenever he accidentally touched my skin I felt as if I had been burnt. I quickly moved my hand out of the way, and he seemed angered by my reaction.

On the third day Guy came to me during the night. He opened the door and stood framed in the doorway. He was wearing a dressing gown. Even though I was now wary and mistrustful of him, and unsure of his integrity, my body craved him from across the empty room. He had come because my body had called to him. I felt my mouth dry with empty longing. I watched him prowl into the room. The restless energy made heat trickle into my belly.

The breath rushed past my lips. Damn it to hell, I wanted this man. I wanted him so bad I felt as if my insides were melting.

I looked at him with wide wanting eyes.

Gently, he traced the outline of my mouth. My lips parted as he pulled the blankets away and his eyes shot down to where my nightgown had ridden up my thighs. Tenderly, he pushed it higher up and gazed down at the triangle of lace stretched between my hip bones. He pulled my panties down my thighs, and very gently over my swollen ankle. Then he climbed into my bed and opened my legs.

'God damn it, Lena, you gave me such a fucking scare,' he muttered hoarsely and dipping his head put his mouth on my clit and sucked the way a man dying of thirst would at a sweet fountain. His fingers drove into me and pumped so fast my body writhed and thrashed like a caught fish. I utterly forgot everything but him. I grasped his hair and curled my legs forward, pulling his face toward my flesh. I wrapped my thighs tightly around his head, and ground my open sex against his mouth, suffocating and smothering him. Waves of sensations poured through me. I moaned and shuddered through my orgasm.

He rolled my slack body to one side and lay down behind me. Arms encircled my waist.

'I want you to take this cock so deep it feels as if it is coming out of your mouth,' he said and curled my legs toward my chest so his erection nestled against my wetness. Then he impaled me.

'Oh,' I gasped.

Before I could get my breath back he punched deeper. And the stray thought in my empty head—he was home. Finally.

'Did you miss my cock?'

'Yes.' I squeezed the hard shaft inside me.

'Good, because I fucking missed your cunt.'

He pumped gently, in time to a slow, sultry rhythm. I could feel his heart beat, and the subtle waves of heat coming from his pores released a secret dream I had always had. His fingers moved between my legs and began to play within my wet folds.

I felt the cold, smooth mask against my temple and his lashes brush my cheek. Along the boundaries of my body every line and follicle of hair embedded in his skin whispered their truth to me and made my heart ache with longing. The gentle rasp of his breathing teased my ears. 'Now do you believe me?' they seemed to say.

The shadows in my mind came alive and I was overcome by the absolute conviction that I did truly belong to him. He had not just bought my body but my heart and my soul. I was his. I was always meant to be his. From the very day I was born. It sounded like a fable to my rational mind. But it was the truth. My truth.

*****

December came and everybody began to talk about Christmas. They seemed so excited. I listened with wonder. It sounded like a very special time. Christmas in Russia was celebrated on the seventh of January and we did not consider it as important as the New Year or Easter celebrations. My mother had told me that in Moscow they put up fir trees and decorated them with tinsel and lights.

I listened quietly to their plans. Their traditions seemed so different. Mrs. Littlebell was baking fruitcakes and storing them in airtight containers. Ren was talking about putting up a Christmas tree. Misty was getting decorations in for it.

'Will we have a Christmas tree here?' I asked.

'Well, Guy doesn't celebrate Christmas, but we always have a small one here in the breakfast room. We put all our presents underneath the tree, and we exchange them on Christmas morning. Then Mrs. Littlebell makes us all a very special Christmas dinner with a huge turkey that we never manage to finish.'

I frowned. 'Do we all exchange presents?'

Misty bit her lip. 'Yes, but we know you have no money so you don't have to give us anything.'

I flushed bright red with shame.

*****

At dinner that night I cornered Guy.

'Everybody will be exchanging presents on Christmas day, but I have no money to buy anybody anything.'

'Christmas?' he said slowly, his eyes suddenly blank and bleak. An expression of pain crossed his eyes.

I stared at him, surprised by the sudden raw anguish. 'Don't you celebrate Christmas?'

'No,' he said and then more softly, 'Not anymore.'

'Why?'

He ignored my question. 'So you want to exchange presents with the staff?'

'Yes.'

He nodded, his mouth twisted into a semblance of a smile. 'It's a good idea. Make a list of all the things you want and I'll get my secretary to send them over.'

I smiled happily. I knew exactly what I wanted to get for everyone. 'Can I choose my own wrapping paper?'

He looked at me, surprised. 'You want to wrap your own presents?'

'Of course.'

'Why?'

'Because it'll be fun.'

'I see. Do you like Christmas?'

'Yes, I'm really looking forward to the whole thing. My family never really celebrated Christmas. We never had presents and we certainly never had a Christmas tree, even though we lived next door to a fir forest. Misty said that we'll be having a small tree in the breakfast room. And we're all going to put our presents underneath it. And we're going to have a turkey dinner. Do you want to join us?' I asked excitedly.

For a moment he said nothing, simply stared at me. Then: 'It might not be such a good idea. But you go ahead and have fun.'

*****

So it was a great and wonderful surprise when two days later a twenty foot Christmas tree arrived on a bright red tractor that actually looked very much like Santa's sleigh.

We all went out to watch the tree being unloaded by four men. Mrs. Littlebell thought it was madness, Misty and I were beside ourselves with excitement, and Ceba growled at the tree. Getting the tree into the middle hall was the easy part. Getting it up on the tree base made of strong, thick, angled struts took not only the four men, but Ren and Mr. Fellowes too. At last it was up.

After they had switched on the fairy lights to make sure everything was working properly, they left, and Misty and I giggled like two schoolgirls. It changed the atmosphere of the whole place and suddenly the castle was no longer gloomy and dark, but like a fairy tale palace. Coming down the stairs to dinner in my long white dress I felt like a fairy tale princess.

Chapter 23

It was a week before Christmas. Mrs. Littlebell had made mince pies and begun to prepare some of the delicacies that we would be having on Christmas day. The Christmas decorations that Misty had ordered had arrived and we were nearly done with the breakfast room when we ran out of greenery, just before we reached the limestone fireplace.

'It doesn't matter,' Misty said.

But I remembered that I had seen green lace in Isabella's room. It would just fill that little space perfectly. So I ran up to her room and was pulling the lace out of the box by the fireplace, when I realized that the draft coming from the fireplace was not cold but warm. I then noticed something else strange. Unlike the other fireplaces in the castle there were no soot marks around the stone. I hunkered down low to the ground and looked up the chimney and was shocked to see an opening on the opposite wall. If I crawled into the chimney and half stood I would be able to see what was inside the dark entrance.

Filled with a sense of adventure and excitement that I might have found something that no one else knew about, I crawled into the small space and half stood. To my surprise it was a secret passageway. It was full of cobwebs and dark.

I went back to my room to find a torchlight then went back and levered myself into the darkness. I crawled along the small square tunnel for what must have been about five minutes until I came to another intersecting passageway. This one was bigger and you could stand in it. I dropped into it and followed it until I came upon what looked like a wooden door. I found the handle, opened it and realized that it was a door hidden behind a large tapestry.

I pushed the tapestry away from the entrance, walked out of the side of it and found myself in a part of the castle I had never been in. The room was not large and the floor was made of flagstones. There was church paraphernalia all around. I opened a wooden door and then I was standing in some sort of a chapel. I walked out of the chapel and came upon a circular staircase.

I climbed it until I reached the first floor. I put my hand on the handle of the door and suddenly I felt a cold hand on me. It shocked me and made all the hair on my hand rise. After that I would always wonder what would have happened if I had heeded that warning hand. If I had not insisted on opening that door. What would my life have been like if I had not peeked at the crane making silk?

I opened the door.

And the strangest sight met my eyes.

My mouth dropped open. This was far worse, much worse than a crane making silk out of its own feathers. The thick curtains were all drawn even though it was daylight outside and the room was dimly lit with restful bluish lights. There were all kinds of blinking machines and medical equipment, almost like a hospital room.

There were two metal beds with railing on the sides and two occupants on them. One was smaller and the other fully grown. Both were female, hairless and grotesquely disfigured beyond anything I had ever seen. Their eyelids seemed to have been sewn shut.

A scream tore through me.

I clapped my mouth. I did not mean to scream.

But the two figures on the bed were oblivious to me. My breath came in spurts. With my heart hammering in my chest I walked closer to the two monstrously scarred figures. Numerous tubes flowed out of them. The room was filled with the artificial sound of their machines breathing for them.

As I stared at them in shock, the door flung open and Guy stood there. The blood drained from my face. I knew then. I had wandered into the forbidden west tower. I had gone where I should not have.

My first reaction was that of a child caught doing something wrong. I began to babble my explanation. 'I didn't know this was the west tower. I followed a secret passageway. I'm sorry, I... I'll just go back the way I came. I haven't touched anything.'

He stared at me dully.

I stopped speaking.

'Meet Meredith, my wife, and Tia, my daughter.'

I felt my eyes widen.

'We were going to a Christmas party. We had taken two cars because I wasn't staying long. It was one of Meredith's friends so she led the way. It happened so fast—suddenly an oncoming vehicle plowed into their car. It was no ordinary accident. They hit a truck carrying oil tanks. There was an explosion. The fire spread quickly.' He winced with the memory. 'I could not get them out in time.'

His hands clenched into fists.

'For more than twelve weeks doctors and nurses grafted the skin from dead people onto them, flushed gallons of medicated fluids and electrolytes through their bodies, vacuumed the soot from their lungs, stuck pins into their flesh to hold together their shattered bones, covered their bodies with maggots that ate away at the dead skin and tissue, ripped away sheets of their flesh over and over again, and fought to keep their organs from shutting down. But medicine can't do any more for them. So I brought them here. Here they are safe from all harm and cared for by Misty.'

There was nothing I could do or say. My mind was a total blank.

'Do you think they are ugly?' His voice was soft and wheedling.

I shook my head, but it was a lie. Of course they were. Horribly ugly. It was almost impossible to look at such destruction and not recoil in horror. They were so scarred and twisted they were barely human.

'Well, my darling, I am as much a beast as they are,' he said, and took off his mask.

Beyond the deep, dark penetrating eyes, and the long curling eyelashes, his chiseled face was so earth-shatteringly handsome he hardly looked real. But that was only one side of his face. The other was a gnarled mess of gored, deformed flesh. Most of his cheek was white, red, uneven, and totally cooked through.

He touched his cheek with his good hand. 'I had to press my face into red-hot burning metal and hold it there while it scorched through my skin, muscle, tendons, and smoldered down to my bone to get Tia out.'

My mouth dropped open. But not for the reason he thought. Not with horror. With wonder. I realized instantly that the scars didn't matter. I didn't care. I loved him with all my being. And he was not ugly. Not at all.

But in a flash I saw him become so desolate, so inconsolable that it shocked me to the marrow. Just as I froze when my father boiled my mother's hand, I froze then. In those few seconds our lives changed.

Misty burst into the room. She was panting hard. She must have run up the stairs. She did not look at me. Her whole attention was on Guy. It was as if she was waiting for him to say something. He turned away from me and slammed his forearms on the wall, his shoulders, big and solid, heaving as he muttered, 'Do it.'

Do what? I stared at him.

Refusing to look at me he opened the door and walked out.

I couldn't understand what was happening. I couldn't react. I was in a state of shock. Everything felt like it was happening too fast. Like being underwater. I opened my mouth and I felt Misty take hold of my upper arm. I turned around to look at her, and couldn't believe my eyes.

She was holding a syringe.

Even then I couldn't react. 'What are you doing?' I asked stupidly.

She inserted the needle into my flesh with expert precision. Misty was a nurse, I gathered in wonder. The needle exited my flesh. My eyes traveled up to her.

'I love him,' I whispered to her. 'Please... Misty, don't let him send me away... Please don't... Help me...' And then a jarring thought. I looked at her without real comprehension. 'You had the needle ready.'

'I *always* knew you would end up here,' she said very softly, and her eyes were glittering with hate.

Shocked, I hung onto her, but the ability to grasp had left me; my fingers were becoming like butter, soft and melting. She gently rubbed my back, the action totally at odds with the hatred shining in her eyes. My last thought was silly—but we were supposed to exchange presents on Christmas day.

Then blackness came. But the blackness was soft and deep.

And you let her go...

You see her when you fall asleep,
But never to touch and never to keep,
'Cause you loved her too much
And you dived too deep.
—Passenger, 'Let Her Go'
http://bit.ly/1j1JzPJ

Chapter 24

The first thing I saw when I opened my eyes was a woman's face. She was staring at me curiously, but as soon as our eyes met she shifted hers away. I was slumped against a glass window. I realized immediately that I was in a moving train. In a panic I looked out of the window and saw rolling countryside. My mouth felt cottony.

I looked at myself. I was dressed in the same clothes as last night, but I was also wearing my blue coat. Feeling dazed I glanced around me. There was no bag or suitcase. I did not even have a change of clothing. I patted my jeans pockets on the coat and my jeans. I pulled it out. It was a British passport. I opened it. The passport was mine: it bore my picture and my name and showed my nationality as British. I held it tightly in my hand. I had been cast away with no money at all. Not even my lace. And yet he had left me with a passport. Why the passport?

I looked again at the woman opposite me. She was now pretending to look out of the window. She had curly ginger hair and a thin, long nose.

'Excuse me,' I said, my voice sounding thick and frightened. 'Can you tell me where this train is going to?'

She gave me a funny look. 'Last stop is London.'

'London,' I repeated softly. I bit my lip. 'Do you know what station I got on at?'

She looked at me suspiciously. 'No, you were already here when I got on.'

I covered my face with my hands. What on earth was I going to do now? How was I going to manage? I had no money. I knew nothing about London. I'd end up on the street in the middle of winter. I had seen on TV how dangerous the streets were. The train was stopping. The woman opposite me stood up. I felt like clutching her hand. She seemed like my only hope. But I remained sitting and she left the carriage. How could he? How could he do something so heartless to me? I began to cry. A middle-aged woman from the seat across the aisle got up from her seat and came and took the seat the ginger-haired woman had vacated.

'What's wrong, my dear?' she asked softly. She had kind blue eyes, rosy cheeks, and short brown hair. There was an old-fashioned brooch with dull stones pinned on the lapel of her collar.

Somehow I trusted her. 'I seem to be homeless and penniless,' I admitted.

'Oh dear,' she said.

'Did you see what stop I got on at?'

'I'm afraid not, dear. You were already on and fast asleep when I got on.'

'Would you know where I could find shelter and work? I'd be willing to work very hard just for food and shelter.'

'Well, there are shelters for homeless people dotted about London, but you don't want to go there, my dear. You seem to be such a gentle little thing. They are a rough, tough crowd. You wouldn't fare too well; they'd steal your shoes from under your feet.' She looked at me as if considering something in her mind. Eventually she smiled and said, 'Well, I shouldn't really. My daughter is always telling me off for picking up strays and waifs from the streets, but, I suppose, you could come and stay at my place for a few days. My daughter is away at university and you can stay in her room for a bit.'

I stared at her, not daring to believe my ears or my luck.

'Do you mean live in your house?'

She nodded with an encouraging smile. 'Yes, come and stay with me until you sort yourself out.'

I wanted to fling my hands around her neck and kiss her. And I did. She went pink with embarrassment. 'It's not a big flat, but it's clean and safe.'

'How kind of you. Thank you. Thank you.'

She waved my effusive thanks away. 'It's nothing, my dear.'

'How can I ever thank you?' I choked.

'Oh, don't worry about that. Tonight I will call my son and ask him about helping you to find a job. Waiting jobs are plentiful in London.' She winked. 'And with you being such a pretty thing I'm sure you will make a fortune in tips.'

'Oh... I don't even know your name,' I said.

She laughed. 'I'm Margaret Mann, but just call me Margaret.'

'And I'm Lena.'

'What a lovely name,' she said and opening her handbag took out a bar of chocolate. 'Are you hungry?'

I realized I was starving. 'Yes, please.'

She brought out a sandwich, too, from her voluminous handbag. 'Here, you might as well have this as well. I thought I might get a little peckish, but I'm not.'

The trip into London was uneventful. I ate the sandwich in a daze. It was the most incredible luck. And Margaret deliberately did not pry into my affairs but talked pleasantly about the friend up north that she had stayed the weekend with and about her daughter who was reading law at university. She pointed out the towns we passed and told me a little about them too. I had no time to think of Guy. He lay at the back of my mind the way a throbbing pain does.

Finally, the train came to a stop at Paddington. A ticket inspector was waiting at the end of the platform. Margaret tried to explain to him that I had lost my ticket, but he shook his head firmly. Margaret would have to pay at the counter. So poor Margaret had to pay the full fare for me. We put our tickets through a machine and the machine opened its flaps and let us through. I stood in that vast station in awe, my mouth open.

It was so busy. So alive.

I had never seen anything like it before. I couldn't breathe. I couldn't talk. It was such a shock to my system. It was sensory overload. The smells, the sounds, the sights. There were people of all races and they milled around me like busy ants. And I loved it. Here, no one knew me. I was invisible—another body in the crush of bodies. Right then and there I knew. I was never going to live in Russia again.

'Follow me,' Margaret said confidently, and took me down the Underground system where there were even more swarms of people. I fingered the passport in my jacket pocket and told myself again and again that everything would be all right.

Margaret lived in Bayswater. As she had warned me it was a tiny two bedroom flat. She put her key in the door, pushed it open, and said, 'We're home.'

And I knew then that it would be all right. I would survive.

The flat was scrupulously clean. She showed me to a room with a single bed. 'This is where you will sleep.' She went to the cupboard and, opening it, said, 'These are all the clothes that my daughter didn't deem good enough to take with her, so I don't think she would mind if you wore them. She is shorter than you but about the same size. Why don't you take a shower while I make some tea for us?'

While I was in the shower I cried. I cried because I had frozen and I had not told him I loved him, I cried because of the pain I had seen in his eyes, I cried because Misty had betrayed me, and most of all I cried because I was frightened that I would never see Guy again.

*****

Margaret's son, Brian, came around that evening. He was only a few years older than me. He had a friend who owned an Italian restaurant. He grinned at me.

'You're one lucky girl, Lena. A waitress walked out yesterday and he's desperate to replace her since Christmas is a busy time.'

'I don't have any experience,' I said worriedly.

'These things are easy. You can learn on the job. Anyway you have to start somewhere.'

'All right.'

'He'll be there now. Come with me, I'll introduce you.'

He took me to a small Italian restaurant in a cobbled side street. It had red and white checked curtains and tablecloths. Inside, it was warm and friendly. I could hear voices speaking in a foreign language coming from the back.

The owner was a round, bespectacled man called Roberto. His hands were very fat and white. He took a sip of espresso and then had to tug out that finger that had become stuck in the circle of the handle.

'Gout,' he told me mournfully. 'Very painful. I used to be able to run faster than a gazelle, but no more. Can you run?'

'Yes, I can run. Very fast.'

He smiled. 'Have you got a white blouse and a black skirt?'

'I will have them by tomorrow.'

'Good, then you can start tomorrow. Come in at ten a.m.'

'That's it?'

'I'm not one for talking. Tomorrow we will try you out. Rosella will show you what to do and we'll see how it goes.'

I grinned. 'Thank you so much.'

'Brian tells me you are from Russia.'

'I am.' At that reminder I immediately thought of my brother. I had to start saving money. I would write to him tonight and tell him of my change of circumstances. Soon I would be able to go to Russia and fetch him. Now that I knew I could definitely survive on my own.

'Part of the Russian mafia?' he asked jokingly.

I didn't get the joke. I just shook my head.

'Good. We have enough mafia in Italy.' He moved his legs and winced with pain. 'Gout,' he explained again. 'Very painful.'

A man dressed in a chef's uniform came out of the swing door of the kitchen and put a large plate of what looked to be lamb shank, potatoes and vegetables in front of Roberto.

'I'll see you tomorrow,' he said, picking up his knife and fork.

After Brian took me back to Margaret's flat, she and I searched through Carrie's cupboard. As it turned out she did own a simple white blouse and a black skirt. It did not reach my knees, but Margaret winked and assured me the shorter the skirt, the higher the tips.

Margaret and I had an early dinner. It was overcooked and pretty tasteless compared to Mrs. Littlebell's cuisine, but I was very grateful and cleaned the plate. Afterwards Margaret invited me to sit and watch TV with her, but I said I was tired and asked if she had writing paper and an envelope. She rummaged about in a drawer and gave me a pad and an envelope. I thanked her and went back to my new room.

I sat on the bed and wrote to Nikolai. I told him I was free. I was now living in London and in a few months' time I was coming for him. We would live together in London. I folded my letter and put it into the envelope. After that I crawled into bed.

I closed my eyes and all I could see was Guy—the expression on his face. He had thought he repulsed me. I had not been repulsed. Not in the slightest. In fact, I had expected far worse after seeing his wife and child, and I was actually stunned by the stern beauty of one side of his face. I wondered what he might be doing and suddenly, I felt so lost and I missed him so much that I stuck my head under the pillow and sobbed myself to sleep.

Chapter 25

Hawke

The night was fading. Another empty soul-destroying day was waiting in the wings. I remembered how she used to make the night last forever. I opened the door and entered her room. The windows were shut, the curtains drawn. It was as quiet as a graveyard. A wave of such sadness swept over me that I leaned against a wall and breathed slowly. In my hand I held a bottle of brandy and a glass. It always helped to anesthetize my mind. With it I no longer smelt them burning, or heard their screams, or saw the flames licking at their skin, their flesh. Burning. Burning. Burning. While I tore my hands on mangled steel.

I gripped the bottle and glass tightly.

My eyes roamed the space. So much of her was still locked in this room. She had found an old music system from somewhere and had brought it here. She had picked some flowers from the gardens and stuck them in a blue vase. She had put out a dress to wear that evening for dinner. It lay on the bed. I walked over to it. It was a pretty thing. Some shiny yellow material with black netting on top. There were little green flowers made of green material scattered on the skirt of the dress and becoming more and more dense as it got closer to the hemline.

I reached out and touched it. The twist of pain was sudden, unexpected, and violent. It felt as if I was being ripped apart. The feeling was beyond animalistic.

If only she had not found the secret passageway. I had wanted to keep her a little longer. I had promised to let her go in a year. Fuck it. Who was I kidding? I had wanted to keep her forever. But I was only fooling myself. Sooner or later she would have seen me without my mask. Of course, she could never have loved me. Not the monster that I am.

I breathed out slowly and walked away from the dress and went toward the cassette player. On the way I saw my reflection in the mirror. I stopped and looked at myself. Surprised. Not by my scars. Not by the hideousness of my reflection, but by my eyes. At how sunken and haunted they looked. I looked away and continued toward the player.

I looked at the music she had collected. Old songs from the sixties and seventies. There was already a tape in the machine. I clicked play.

'Love Hurts' by the Everly Brothers.

The sound was bad, tinny, and scratchy. This was not music. It hurt my ear. I wanted to switch it off and yet she had found pleasure even in this scratchy music. This was the last thing she had listened to.

I felt sorry for her then. Poor thing. She was just a child. So innocent and yet so brave. I had learned from her. How much I had learned from her. She had asked only one thing of me. How badly I had treated her. I was a fucking selfish bastard. I should have taken her out. I should have got her a good music system. I could have made her life so much better. It would have cost me nothing. Instead I condemned her to wander around this dark and depressing castle. Not that she complained. She was always so ready to laugh. Ready to find joy in the smallest thing. I was too harsh and too cold with her. I never showed her love. I was afraid to show her love.

The music changed. Dolly Parton crooned, '*I will always love you. I hope life treats you kind and I hope you have all you ever dreamed of.*'

I hated country singers, but that night her voice tore at my insides. I went and sat on the bed and I poured myself a glass and threw it down my throat. Then I poured another glass, and another, and another. I looked at the bottle. Half gone. I lay down on the bed and stared at the canopy and knew a great emptiness inside me. Outside, it began to rain.

'Oh, Lena, Lena, Lena,' I whispered, and thought of her tender body reaching for me. The memory rolled like thunder across my mind. I had let a precious thing slip between my fingers. I thought I was holding on tight, but she had slipped out like sand.

I remembered her again, telling me about the ghost she had befriended. A smile came to my lips at the memory. What a child she was. She must have been really lonely to have created a ghost. Suddenly the door opened and Misty walked in. She stopped when she saw me.

I jack-knifed upwards, my stomach in knots. 'What is it? What's wrong?'

She shook her head. 'Nothing is wrong. They are both fine.'

I rubbed the side of my head. 'What are you doing here?'

'I saw the light...' She let her voice trail away.

'Yeah, it's just me.'

'Guy?'

'Yeah?'

'I miss her too.'

I closed my eyes. When I opened them she had come closer. She was wearing a green dress with round metal cut-outs at the waist and around the hemline. It was too tight around her breasts. Her nipples showed through. I averted my eyes quickly. She sat on the bed beside me and looked into my eyes. She was wearing make-up. I had never noticed what pretty eyes she had. Her hand reached out and covered mine. I looked down at it. How small it was compared to mine.

'She was my best friend.'

I looked up and met her eyes. What was in her eyes was different from what her words were telling me. My alcohol-addled brain caught her perfume.

'You are wearing Lena's perfume,' I whispered. My voice was shocked and raw. It felt wrong. The idea made my flesh creep. I had specially commissioned that perfume for my Lena.

'Yes, it reminds me of her.'

She put her hand on my upper arm. I felt my muscles contract with revulsion. She mistook the response and turning her head suddenly let her mouth fall on mine. The glass in my hand crashed to the floor. My hands were suddenly curled around her upper arms and she was moving very fast away from me. She fell back onto the bed and stared up at me, breathing hard. Her hands touched her mouth.

'Fuck me. Use me like you did her,' she said.

I stood and looked at her, her hair spread on the bed, her short dress ridden high up her thighs, her top button unbuttoned, her hand stroking the one exposed naked breast. I watched her pinch her own nipple and gasp. I watched her part her thighs and show me her freshly shaven pussy. It was a good offer, but she was not my Lena.

I reached down and closed her legs. 'I can't, Misty. I'm sorry,' I said, and began to walk away.

From the tape recorder Eric Carmen's rich voice sang 'All By Myself'. *'Don't wanna be all by myself. Anymore.'*

'She never wanted you. In fact, she hated your touch,' she called out.

I stopped. Her words chilled my soul. I never knew I could feel so empty and so lost. Now I knew the truth. She never wanted me. My knees felt stiff as if they were made of iron or some inflexible material. But turn I must. I had been so stupid. So blind. I should have known. My heart filled with regret. I had put the chicken in the care of the fox. I had defeated myself.

When I turned around to look at her my face was cold and utterly indifferent. I looked into her pretty eyes. I had never really looked before. I caught the glimmer of poison, but at the expression on my face, a new fear crept into her face.

'You have mistaken my generosity for weakness.'

'I'm sorry,' she cried quickly. 'I didn't mean to say that. I love you.' Her voice was passionate.

'Don't,' I said, my voice icy. 'You are relieved of all your duties as of now. I want you out in the morning. You will be paid two months' salary in lieu of notice.'

'You can't do that. What about Meredith and Tia?'

'Do not even go near them,' I grated. Even hearing their names on her lips infuriated me.

I left her. My jaw was tight, my heart was broken. Truly broken. Filled with the dull sensation that I didn't want to go on, but of course, I would.

I had lost her, and it was my own damn fault.

Chapter 26

Lena

When I woke in the morning I didn't feel refreshed or energized. My eyes were red and swollen and I looked pale. I showered quickly, dressed in the white top and black skirt, put my hair into one neat plait down my back, and slipped into the only pair of shoes I now owned, which were thankfully my sensible black shoes, and I was ready. I went into the kitchen and Margaret was rooting about in the fridge.

'Sit down and I'll make you breakfast,' she said.

'You don't have to make me breakfast, Margaret. You have already been too kind. When I get my first wages I am going to pay you back.'

She brought her head out of the fridge. 'Oh, Lena. You don't know what a pleasure it is for me to have you stay in my home. I am an old woman now. My children hardly come around and you are like a breath of fresh air in this tired old flat. Please, never talk about paying me back.'

I looked at her uncertainly.

She went to a drawer, opened it, and took two spoons out. She opened the freezer and put the spoons on its icy floor, then she turned back to me.

'What are the spoons for?' I asked.

'They are for your eyes. You can't go to work on your first day and look like you have been crying your eyes out. Come and sit down,' she said.

I slumped into a chair. In truth I felt miserable. Disaster had been averted but my heart was breaking. Guy had abandoned me just like that. With just my passport. Not even a penny. He didn't care at all. If Margaret had not helped me, God knows where I would have spent the night, or even what would have happened to me. I fought back the tears at his callousness.

'There, there,' Margaret said and, coming to me, patted my hand.

'Oh! Margaret,' I sobbed. What could I tell her? That I had fallen madly in love with a man who cared so little that he had thrown me in a train heading for London without so much as a dime?

'Listen,' Margaret said firmly. 'You are alive and you are so incredibly young. No matter what has happened or gone on before this, you can start fresh. No one knows your past, or what you have done. Let this be a new beginning for you.' She handed me a paper napkin.

'Thank you,' I sniffed.

'Dry your tears, Lena. You have so much.'

It was not true that I had so much, but I had Nikolai. I made a massive effort to stop sobbing then. 'Will you post an important letter for me, Margaret?' I asked.

She smiled. 'Of course I will.'

'Thank you so much.'

She opened the freezer, took out the spoons and came toward me. 'Rest the backs on your eyelids while I prepare breakfast. It will bring the swelling and redness down.'

I sat with the cold metal on my eyelids while she prepared eggs, warmed up half a can of baked beans and made two slices of toast. After we had eaten she insisted on coming with me to the restaurant.

'London is a maze. You'll get lost on your own,' she said.

And to be perfectly honest I was truly glad she came because she showed me the way the Underground worked and bought me a weekly ticket.

I turned to her. 'In all my life I don't think I have ever met anyone as kind and as generous as you.'

A shadow passed over her face, but all she said was, 'Nothing gives me more pleasure than helping you, child.'

We parted at the entrance to the restaurant. 'Do you want me to come pick you up at the end of your shift?'

I shook my head. 'I think I know how to find my way home.'

'All right, dear. I'll see you at home. Good luck now.'

I pushed open the restaurant door feeling nervous. What if I dropped food on a customer or made a mistake with a bill? Roberto was not around, but a young woman was behind the bar. She smiled widely at me.

'I'm Rosella. You must be Lena,' she said. 'Roberto described you well.'

'Oh, what did he say?'

'He said you have the face of an angel.'

I blushed and Rosella laughed. 'You've never worked in a restaurant before, right?'

I nodded.

'No problem. It's very easy. Let me introduce you to everybody first. Remember, they are all Italian and they will all try to sleep with you. Just ignore them, unless you want to, that is. But whatever you do, don't ever sleep with the chef. He is totally crazy.'

She took me around the back and introduced me to everyone. As she had predicted they all looked at me with hot, interested eyes. Thirty minutes later the waiters arrived. Rosella made it easy by giving me small jobs—filling the pepper and salt pots, laying the tables, folding napkins. By the time the first customer arrived I felt quite comfortable standing in my position behind the bar polishing glasses and watching her greet and seat them and hand them their menus.

Lunchtime passed as a busy blur. I was kept on my feet and when the last customer left, Marco, one of the waiters, told me I had done well.

'Really?' I asked, pleased.

'He's just trying to get into your pants, but you did do well,' Rosella told me.

'Fuck off,' Marco said to her.

She ignored him. 'See you this evening at five,' she told me, shrugging into her coat.

'What time do we finish at night?'

'Depends on the last customer.'

'But I have to leave before the last train,' I said.

'Don't worry,' Marco offered. 'I'll take you home.'

Rosella looked at him, and then at me, and shrugged. 'There's your lift.'

'Thank you, Marco,' I said quietly.

But when I told Margaret she was not happy. 'You don't know him from Adam. No, no, that's a bad idea. I'll ask Brian to pick you up.'

And though I protested she wouldn't hear different. Brian didn't seem to mind either.

*****

I'd been working at Basilico for two days when a man came into the restaurant. It was lunchtime and he was alone. His hair had been oiled and sculpted into perfect finger waves. He wore a cream shirt, an olive

business jacket, and a pair of jeans. After his food had been cleared away he called me to his table.

'What's your name?' he drawled.

'Lena.'

'Would you like to become a model, Lena?'

'What? Like in a magazine?'

'Yeah, like in a magazine.'

For a moment I was dumbfounded and then I found my voice. 'Yes.'

'Good. In that case there is a casting session tomorrow at three p.m. Here.' He took a card out of his jacket and held it out to me. I took the card and looked at it.

Models101 it was called, and the address was Macklin Street.

'Arrive earlier than three p.m. Put your hair in a ponytail, wear skinny black or dark blue jeans, a form-fitting tank top in a solid color, high heels and no make-up. Got it? Can I take a quick photo?' he asked taking his mobile phone out of his jacket pocket.

'OK.'

'Don't pout and don't smile,' he instructed and clicked. He looked at the photo with narrowed, detached eyes. 'Brilliant,' he pronounced.

I glanced at Rosella and she raised her eyebrows, as in, *What the fuck are you doing?*

'Thanks,' I said quickly, and with a thrill of excitement I left him. Models make more money than waitresses, which meant the sooner I could get Nikolai away from my father.

I asked Rosella if I could have the next afternoon off instead of Thursday and Marco immediately said he would exchange shifts with me. I smiled gratefully at him.

That evening I found that Carrie had a tank top in one solid color. A pair of skinny jeans that were too short, but after I teamed them with high heels they simply looked like ankle-length jeans.

*****

'Do you think I look right?' I asked Margaret. She was sitting at her dining table flipping through a magazine, but she was dressed in a brown suit as if she was going out.

'You'd look divine in a sack,' she said with a smile.

'Why are you all dressed?' I asked her.

'I'm going with you,' she informed me.

'Oh, I don't know if I am allowed to bring anyone with me.'

'Don't you worry, chaperones are the norm in the modeling business. This is a sleazy business and you're just a child. I don't want anyone thinking you are alone and can be taken advantage of.'

I grinned at her. 'OK, that will be great. Thanks, Margaret.'

Together we took the Tube to Holborn Station, walked down Holborn High Street, took a left at Newton Street, then a right turn into Macklin Street. It was a one-way back street. We had to go through a blue entrance and up a set of stairs to 13 Macklin Street. I climbed them with my heart in my throat. As my mother would have said, there was a whole bag of chinchillas in my stomach. At the next landing I saw the black on lilac sign that read Models101, and beside it a set of glass double doors. I could see a white reception desk. It looked very posh. It felt like the big time. Even though Brian had done some research and told me that Models101 was the agency of the moment, and what to expect, some part of me had not believed that it was all real. That a real model scout for Models101 had spotted me working in a restaurant and asked me to a real casting. That was the stuff fairy tales were made of.

Brian had told us to go early for the casting since the rules of casting were that anybody not seen inside the allotted hour would be sent home. Being early assured that you would be seen first. He had told me that it would most probably be a pre-interview, and had very subtly hinted that there was a rather large possibility that I would be sent home with the polite message that the agency would call me if anything came up. And that was probably a bad sign. Or if I was very lucky and had the right face I would be sent in to see the owner of the agency. A powerful woman called Georgina Carangi. She was known in the industry simply as Geo.

But there were no other girls waiting in the tastefully decorated reception area. And instead of the pre-interview I was immediately whisked away by the receptionist to see the boss of the show—Geo. I followed the receptionist but turned back to widen my eyes at Margaret. She grinned irrepressibly like a child, pulled her shoulders up to her ears, and mouthed, 'Good luck.' Outside the dragon's lair, I wiped my sweaty palms on the sides of my jeans and went to meet my fate.

It was a big room full of windows. A thin, dark-haired woman was seated behind an ornate white desk elegantly smoking a cigarette when I entered. She killed the cigarette expertly, without looking at what she was doing. Smoke swirled around her. She was the stuff legends were made of. She made a small beckoning movement with the fingers of her right hand.

It was time to strut my stuff, and strangely I found it easy. I thought of Guy and did it for Nikolai. I raised my chin, pushed my chest out, and slowly glided in, long legs first. I stopped in the middle of the room and waited.

The swirling smoke cleared and I saw her formidable eyes. They were dark and shone with barely suppressed excitement. She leaned back in her chair, flashed a mysterious smile, and let her gaze travel appraisingly down my body. Then she returned her impassive eyes to mine.

'You're not English. Where are you from?' She had a voice like sandpaper.

'Russia.' Shit. My passport claimed I was British.

She smiled very slowly. 'Luckily for you the only things the world will still accept from Russia are petroleum, caviar and long-legged models.'

I attempted a natural smile and failed.

'Turn around,' she instructed.

I did. Slowly.

'Face me again.'

I turned around.

'You'll do very nicely,' she said.

And I broke into a huge grin.

'You won't be doing any Victoria's Secret gigs with those breasts,' she warned, 'but there's work for those legs. A lot of work.'

All I heard was 'A lot of work.'

'Sit down and let's talk,' she said, reaching for her cigarette box.

I was so happy I almost skipped toward her.

On the spot she took me on. She called someone on the phone and told the person on the other end to bring in a contract. A heavily pregnant woman came in with a thin sheaf of papers and handed the document over to me. I took it in a daze.

'Have a look over it or get a lawyer to look at it for you,' Geo said, killing another cigarette. 'Then sign it and make another appointment to see me. You could have a very brilliant future in modeling. And that isn't true of every girl in modeling.' She smiled warmly and, standing up, walked me to the door.

When I walked out of her office Margaret stood and looked at me expectantly. I ran into her arms and hugged her so tightly she squealed.

'Oh, Lena,' she crooned. 'I'm so happy for you.'

Chapter 27

After I signed the four-page document Georgina Carangi and I met again over lunch. She wore sunglasses on her head during the entire lunch and picked at a small salad, cutting the leaves into tiny pieces that she reluctantly slipped into her mouth, as if eating was some sort of intolerable ordeal. In response I tried not to eat so much.

She told me my accent was too thick and that she would be sending me not only for a quick modeling course—you need to walk beautifully—but also for elocution classes.

'The real world needs illusions,' she said.

I nodded silently.

'The first thing I want you to do is a shoot with DZM, a stocking company. The money is lousy, but the photographer is great and very in. French. Get the right photographer behind you and you'll soar. With any luck he will take a picture of you that will look outstanding in your portfolio.'

*****

The photographer's name was Louis Cirilli. He wore skin-tight trousers and had a life-sized black and white photo of a naked man with a very big penis on his studio wall. He looked at me, bit into an apple, and chewed thoughtfully.

'I don't know your history, but you look very vulnerable. It is part of your beauty. As if you can be broken. It is an appeal.' He waved his hands in small circles around his face. 'A beautiful riddle. You know, sexy and dynamite and alive. Like Lady Diana or Marilyn Monroe. If it comes out in the photographs it will be everything.'

I frowned, not sure if I had understood any of that or how to use it.

'Let me explain—every shoot is just looking for that one picture. That one perfect picture. It doesn't matter if it is the first or the last of thousands of shots. But what every photographer will die to capture is that certain faraway look. That certain inner fire.'

With those words of wisdom he sent me off to the make-up artist who began the unbelievably painstaking process of layer upon layer of creams, bases, powders, and pencils that form that impossibly perfect make-up job required for high fashion photography.

'The bright lights will steal all your color, so you need more,' she explained. She also did my back, shoulders, arms, and chest. She even painted my nipples a deeper pink on the off-chance that they could peek out.

It was two whole hours later that I climbed into a see-through blouse and a pair of tights wearing no underwear and six-inch purple heels. I presented myself to Louis nervously.

He clapped his hands. 'Great. OK, get in front of the white screen and move.'

'Move?' I asked.

'Do whatever your body tells you to.'

I stared at him cluelessly.

'Tease me,' he coaxed. 'Make me chase you. Look at me as if you are naked. Tease me like you want me.'

I remembered Geo saying my bum is easily my best asset. I turned away from him and, pushing my ass out, turned my head and looked at him with a fierce expression on my face.

For a second he was surprised. '*That* is how you look at people you want!' Then his eyes lit up as if a light bulb had just gone on under his skin. 'Actually, that *is* perfect...' He began snapping excitedly. 'That's it. Hold it. Fabulous. Fabulous. Fabulous.'

I unbuttoned the see-through blouse and sucked my thumb.

'Great, yes. Face the wind machine. Kick your leg back. Higher, higher. Fabulous, fabulous, fabulous. Laugh, laugh, laugh. Throw your hands forward. That's it. Beautiful. Marvelous.'

After the session he gave me a can of warm Pepsi. His eyes were almost glazed with professional excitement. 'You were *born* to be in front of the camera. The way you move... You know your face, you know your body.

That cannot be learned. You have to be born with that. You were born to be a model. You will leapfrog all the other new faces at Models101 and every other agency. You are about to become the new cheetah of the fashion world,' he predicted.

From that session one stunning image emerged.

Louis sent it to me via courier. He said it was the kind of shot that would stop even the most jaded photographer in his tracks. And it was the strongest picture he had taken of anyone before. It was also, he claimed, the kind of picture that would make my career. I looked at it and it shocked me. I could not believe it was me.

The dark make-up around my eyes made me look ephemeral and sadly seductive, and my legs shot from below seemed flawless and endless. Pleased, I showed it to Geo. She took out her opera glasses and looked at it carefully. Eventually, she looked up and said, 'You are the perfect illusion. You hide the emptiness of every fashion shoot.'

*****

It was after a quiet Christmas with Margaret and her children that Geo sent me to the dark prince of fashion photography. He was, technically, a German baron who had decided to pursue his fascination with strong, sexually charged and often shocking images. *Italian*

Bazaar had hired him for the assignment and the shoot was located at an old ruined French chateau.

I sat in a makeshift dressing room and the make-up artist, a chatty French girl, got on with the long job of painting my face. Afterwards, I slipped into a slinky black mini dress with a plunging neckline and I was ready. The shoot had been set up in one of the bedrooms. The bed had been made with silk sheets and had animal print throws on it. The baron had brought shackles and wanted to shackle me to the bed. I froze at the sight of the irons and chains.

'Come on, come on,' he said impatiently.

His helpers snapped them onto my wrists and my ankles. And then tears began to run down my face. *Oh, Guy! How I miss you. You pushed me away from you, but I haven't forgotten you. I'm still so in love with you.*

One of the make-up girls ran toward me, waving a tissue, shouting, 'You're going to ruin the make-up.'

But the baron said, 'Leave her. She has tiger eyes.' And immediately began clicking furiously.

Afterwards I asked him, 'Tiger eyes? What do you mean?'

'Tiger eyes are perfect and pure. They are like babies' eyes. They have not yet been tainted by their parents' thoughts, or acquired the filtration of how to perceive the world. They are not yet imprisoned by education, culture and religion. Given half the chance they will eat their own shit.'

When the photographs came out they caused an almighty sensation.

'Maybe that is why you photograph so successfully. You have that look. An elusive quality of vulnerability—the face of a little girl and yet you project like a big cat. Full on,' Geo said.

I looked at the image in the magazine spread. Manacled to the bed, I was looking out to the camera. The mascara had run. It was in black and white and it had a quality of timelessness to it. The old chateau with its celestial ceiling, the blonde hair spilling over the side of the Versailles bed. The red lipstick they attributed to Lancôme, but of course was not.

The magazine called it 'crying in a highly provocative way while looking achingly beautiful'. They called me 'a thing of beauty'. They declared me to be without fences. They thought I was 'fragile'. I only saw myself shackled with both my hands over my pubic area, glaring angrily at those who would look at me.

*****

Three weeks later I leapt out of bed at the crack of dawn and ran to the little magazine kiosk in the Tube station. Mr. Patel beamed at me and lifted a magazine up high. I couldn't believe it. There I was staring back at me.

'You're famous,' he said loudly.

And I began to laugh. I laughed like a crazy woman. I grabbed the surprised Mr. Patel and whirled him around in a little mad dance. People started staring. He went dark red with embarrassment. I didn't care. I was so happy. I ran all the way back to Margaret's flat clutching five magazines. One compliments of Mr. Patel and the rest I had bought with my own money.

'I made the cover of *Italian Bazaar*. I made the cover of *Italian Bazaar*,' I screeched.

Margaret opened a bottle of champagne that she had been saving for her daughter's birthday. We had pancakes with maple syrup and champagne.

'My first ever cover,' I said.

After that I made *Vogue* and *Bazaar* and *GQ* but nothing else ever came close to that morning's sparkle. Oh! What a feeling it was. Just me and Margaret in her small flat, the sun pouring in through the window, and both of us talking in hushed, excited voices. But the money was very poor. At this rate it would be a long time before I could get Nikolai out of Russia. I went to see Geo.

'The secret of the fashion industry is that the glamorous magazines that power the fashion world and launch the new faces of the industry pay shit money. Even supermodels get the measly industry standard to do their covers, but inside those covers is where the next Revlon girl, or the next face of Gucci is found. And that is where the real money lies.'

'Right,' I said worriedly.

'Versace is looking for a new face.' She stopped speaking and called someone.

'She has gray almond eyes and blonde hair. And legs. She's got acres of those. You've got to see her.' She listened for a few seconds. 'Tomorrow?' She paused, and looking at me winked, then very sweetly said into the phone, 'I'll send her to you at midday.'

The next day I was on a plane to Milan to turn up at the great Donatella Versace.

'I like you, and I am going to make you famous,' she said gruffly.

That afternoon a reporter called. Things were about to get mad for me. The offers and assignments came pouring in through the bookers' desks. My life changed so dazzlingly fast that I moved through it in a disbelieving daze. The only time the daze went away was when I sat down every night to write to Nikolai and afterwards to think of Guy.

Geo took me out to lunch to talk business. First we talked about the photographers and what I wanted from the business. The truth was I didn't care for the modeling business, or my overnight success. I was not star-struck. This was not the kind of job I loved, or I could ever come to love. Everything and everyone seemed to be so fake and superficial. Only the parties were more extravagant than the flattery. I was only interested in the money I could make. My only goal was getting Nikolai away from Russia.

'You're doing great,' she said. 'The photographers love you. Just keep working with them.' Her plan was for me to work in Europe for a few months. 'I think it will be very good for you. How does Paris sound?'

'Paris?' My head spun. My mother had been to Paris many years before I was born. She said it was the most glamorous place in the world.

'Yes. Have you never been to Paris?'

I shook my head. 'I need to go to Russia first,' I said.

She had never asked me about my past or my private life. Her eyes narrowed.

'I need money. I need to pay for someone to come into this country.'

She frowned. 'Who?'

'My brother.'

She exhaled slowly. 'I'll see what I can do.'

'No, I have to go myself and get him.'

Chapter 28

The taxi pulled up in the dirty road where I had once lived with my family and my heart began to hammer in my chest. I was so excited to see my brother again there was a hard knot in my stomach. It had been there ever since I had boarded the plane.

'I've really, really, really missed you,' I would tell him. Or should I say, 'You didn't believe me, but I've kept my promise. I've come to take you away.'

The driver stopped the car. Brian, who had insisted on coming with me, wished me luck, and I walked to the front door. The house seemed quiet. The door was unlocked so I lifted the metal latch and entered.

The stove was not lit. The house was cold. There was a stillness in the air. Something was wrong. For a moment I paused by the samovar. Memories came pouring back—my mother, my siblings seated around the table eating. And I was filled with feelings of loss and intolerable sadness.

I could see from the window that there was a figure sitting on the recliner chair in the backyard. I recognized him instantly as my father. For a moment I walked to the window and stood watching him. I noticed that the tin of salt left between the windowpanes over winter so that the windows didn't fog in the cold looked as if no one had replaced it for a very long time. The place looked abandoned. I frowned. My hand went to my forehead and rubbed it. The breath I took felt painful.

He has sold my brother. Now it will be so much harder to find him. I opened the back door. My father turned his face. It looked gray and startled. I walked toward him, my shoes crunching on sunflower seed shells.

He peeled another seed and threw the shell any which way.

'Where's Nikolai?' I asked. My voice was strong. The truth was I was never really afraid of him. I obeyed him first because I was afraid for my mother and then because of my brother. There was nothing he could do to me. He had no more power. There was no one to hold over my head.

His eyes grazed my face. I knew instantly that he did not appreciate my tone. 'He is dead,' he said brutally.

His words hit me like a blow to the stomach. It sucked the breath out of me.

He narrowed his eyes at my reaction. 'I told the men who came to ask.'

'How?' I gasped.

'He hanged himself on the day you left.'

I closed my eyes and fought to corral the shock to my system, but it was impossible. I had never even once felt that he had left this world. I had written countless letters. I had dreamt of him. I had thought I could feel him, his presence over thousands of miles. I had never suspected. The connection had never felt as if it was broken. It had never ever crossed my mind that he had been dead for so long. My whole world felt as if it was crumbling. I felt myself sinking to the ground. I will not cry in front of this monster, I thought. I put my palms on the ground and with my legs folded underneath me faced him.

'You've always hated me?'

'Yes.' There was no hesitation in his answer.

'Why?'

He made a careless movement with his shoulder.

'If you hated me so much why did you sell me last?'

'For Nikolai. He told me he would kill himself if I ever sold you.' Even though he had tried to appear nonchalant, Nikolai's death had affected him deeply.

'But you still did it.'

'I didn't believe he had the guts to do it.'

For a moment neither of us spoke. I thought of Nikolai, gentle Nikolai. It was his job to skin the animals my father brought, but he could never do the head. He could never stomach their glassy eyes. It was always me who did the heads. And yet, he had had the courage to take his own life.

'Why did you do it?' I asked him. And in that one sentence was all my hurt and pain. It was about my brother. It was about my mother, my sisters, me. Why did he do what he did? Why did he destroy every single person who loved him? Why was he here alone in a cold, empty house? What good had the money done for him?

He shrugged carelessly and cracked open another seed.

I watched him put it into his mouth and chew it slowly. He did not intend to answer me. I stood slowly. As if I was an old woman. I turned away to leave and then I turned back to him.

'What men?'

'The men that the man who bought you sent.'

I frowned. Confused. Had Guy sent someone to get my brother for me? I turned fully toward my father.

'When did they come?'

'About a month after you left.'

My brain scrambled around trying to assimilate this information. Guy had sent someone and then lied about it, because he did not want me to know that my brother had hanged himself. And that day after I had given him the first envelope he had stroked my hair. There was a strange expression—a pity in his eyes. I remembered it clearly. No wonder he did not send my letters. He should have told me. It was worse like this.

I began to walk away.

'Don't come here again,' my father called out to me. I heard the crack of another sunflower seed split in his mouth. The hiss as it hit the ground.

I had never intended to come back here and he knew that, but even that tiny victory he had to take away from me. He could not even allow me that small decision. I walked into the house and noticed all our chairs. My father had left them against the wall. On my brother's chair was a pile of envelopes. I went and picked them up. The sight of them unopened and unread made me feel sick. It was too late to put things right. The two saddest words in the English dictionary. Too late. And it was too late. Death always made it too late.

Pressing my lips together I ran to the taxi. I could see Brian's face turned in my direction. And then I heard the wind in the apple tree. It was like my mother's whisper. And suddenly I felt as if my brother's young body stood inside mine and ordered me to go back. To where he lay. I walked toward the side of the house. I could see another gravestone beside my mother's grave. I went and sat beside it.

'You should have waited for me,' I whispered woodenly.

I took my shoes off and he was in the grass that tickled my feet. I dug a hole in the ground with my bare hands and buried the letters. Then I went back to the taxi.

'Are you all right?' the taxi driver asked me in Russian.

'Take me back to the station,' I said, too numb to cry. I sat and stared out of the window, my hands covered in the dirt from my brother's grave. One fingernail was broken and bleeding. But I felt no pain.

Chapter 29

I changed after I went to Russia. The model's job is essentially to encourage a lot of people to sleep with her. And the more successful she is, the more products she sells. While I posed and smiled and traveled the world pretending to be that fantasy woman— too young, too thin, too vulnerable—peddled by the fashion world to sell wonderland, I actually felt as if I was the creation of a being who had closed his eyes and dreamed up a woman who most closely resembled dust.

I had lost my entire family and both the people I loved most in my life—my brother and Guy. And the longer the desperate days went on, the more pathologically isolated and lost I felt. I knew I had to either forget Guy or die myself. It felt impossible to carry on with such intense sadness.

One day it got so bad that I found a dark scarf in the cupboard and tied it around my eyes. Immediately the feelings of loss and pain subsided. Suddenly I felt comforted in the darkness and the quiet. At peace I felt my way to my bed and sat on it. A soft contentment stole over me.

'The best place for you is France,' Geo said.

So I went to France.

Jacques came to the airport to meet me. He was a model too. Good-looking, charming, and gay. 'You are to live with me and Helena,' he said.

'Great.'

The flat was small but cheerfully decorated. Helena turned out to be another model signed to the French arm of Models101. She was painfully thin with large, soulful brown eyes. I liked her instantly. I loved her accent and how easily she laughed.

'We are having student food for our first meal together,' she said with her charming accent. We sat down to spaghetti with butter and tomato purée followed by rabbit flambéed with nearly half a bottle of alcohol. I sat with them and for a while the dull ache that was Guy lay quiet.

'Tomorrow I will take you to the Champs-Elysées,' she said. 'You will love it.'

And she was right: I did, until I thought I saw Guy's broad shoulders, and leaving her, I dashed up to him and touched his arm. A stranger turned.

'Excusez-moi, excusez-moi,' I mumbled, and walked back to a surprised Helena.

'Are you all right?' she asked.

'Yes,' I said, but the day was ruined.

*****

That Friday I was scheduled to leave for the south of France to do a bikini shot. Helena looked at me wistfully. 'You are so lucky,' she said.

'Do you want to come with me? It's a private plane so it won't cost any more if you come with me and stay in my room,' I offered.

They sent a limo for us and we climbed in. There was champagne on ice. Helena opened it and we giggled all the way to the airport.

The photographer was a mischievous-looking Italian man. His eyes widened when he saw that I had brought a friend.

'I am a playboy,' he confessed. 'But the word playboy means a different thing in Italy. A playboy is a charming man. Not a bastard who fucks girls and leaves them broken-hearted! No, no, the Italian playboy, he is not so rude or cruel. He falls in love with the girl. He is romantic. He can sleep with ten girls and be in *love* with all ten girls.'

'Good,' I told him, totally unimpressed.

On our first night, Helena stole out of our room, and slept with him. At breakfast he ordered an omelet with truffles for her, and after that she became invisible to him. When we were out to dinner it was sad. She was so beautiful and he was just a fat fuck. All that talk of falling in love with ten women... Just bullshit.

He breathed down my neck.

I smiled politely at him. Work the photographers, Lena.

When we went back to France, Helena was subdued. I didn't know what to say.

*****

Another Christmas passed and I inhaled the crisp January air. I had just returned from an assignment working with Sascha Bourdin, a master photographer, in Seychelles. When I opened the door to the flat, Helena was lying on the couch. There was an empty bottle of red wine on the table. She looked wasted. Her eyes were red and swollen.

'What's the matter, Helena?'

'I'm just so fucking sick of having to suck shriveled cock just to get a gig,' she spat bitterly.

I sat beside her. 'Helena, you are so beautiful. You don't need to do that to get a job.'

'Nobody told you what modeling really is, did they? Not that bitch Carangi. Here's a free lesson for you. Modeling is very glamorous at the top, lucratively tedious at the middle, and unspeakably sleazy at the bottom. Guess where I am?'

She was so bitter and so different from how she usually was, I didn't know how to react.

She looked at me sadly. 'I was in *Vogue* once. Did you know that?'

I shook my head. 'Really?'

'Yes, I was. But I am a whim, you see. They use me once and then they never do again. And it doesn't matter to them that I am discarded like rubbish. It's terrible, don't you think? I'm not big time. Now when I want a job I have to suck a cock.'

'You don't need to suck cock, Helena. I'm not big time either and I don't suck anybody's cock for a job.'

Her head whirled around angrily. 'Maybe that's because you already sucked the right cock.'

I stared at her in shock. Speechless.

Her face changed. She looked horrified. She clapped her hands over her mouth. 'I'm sorry. I shouldn't have said that. I didn't mean it.' Her palms met in front of her mouth in a praying gesture. 'Please don't tell Jacques that I said that.'

'What did you mean by that?' I asked slowly. My voice was cold and distant.

'I didn't mean anything.' She pointed to the bottle of red wine. 'I've been drinking.' She laughed. A high unnatural sound. 'I'm stupid when I am drunk.'

'I won't tell Jacques anything if you tell me what you really meant.'

For a while she stared at me, a crafty look in her eyes, as she was wondering what the best way was to wriggle out of the situation she was in. 'Promise you won't tell him. He will be so mad with me. Neither of us get enough jobs to pay our bills anymore.' She looked frightened.

'I promise not to tell Jacques.'

'All right. We get paid a lot of money to let you live with us. It's Jacques's job to protect you. That's why he follows you around. And that's why he keeps all the men away and why he punched that Greek guy who wouldn't take no for an answer.'

My heart was thudding so hard the blood roared in my ears. 'Who is paying you to house and protect me?'

'We don't know. All we know is every month money appears in our account. It comes from a solicitor's office. A week before you came to France, Jacques was approached by a solicitor, and asked if he wanted the job of housing and protecting a fellow model. He refused to give Jacques any information at all. The job was simple. We were to offer you housing and act as your protectors, but if we revealed this to anyone, the contract would become null and void and we would no longer get paid. So you cannot go and see that solicitor.'

I sat back and leaned against the back of the couch. Helena was saying something else, but I could not concentrate. I stood up.

'Thank you,' she said.

I nodded slowly. 'I have to go to England.'

'Please don't do anything rash.'

'No, this won't in any way affect you. I have something important I have to check out.'

*****

I flew back to England and went to see Margaret. She opened the door with a wide smile. 'Come on in. I was just about to put the kettle on.'

I sat with her at the kitchen table. She poured the tea.

'Margaret?' I said.

'Yes, dear.' She spooned sugar into her cup and stirred it.

'It wasn't by accident that we met on the train, was it?'

Her hands stilled suddenly. Her soft blue eyes fixed on me. She took a deep breath. 'No.'

'Does a solicitor pay you?'

'Yes.'

'Do they still pay you?'

'Every month.'

'You were just supposed to house me?'

'Yes, and help you find your feet.'

'And the job at the restaurant?'

'We were told to take you there.'

'And the modeling job?'

'I had nothing to do with the modeling job. I just accompanied you there. I was only supposed to house you, show you the ropes, and help you adjust to life in London.'

I took a sip of tea. No wonder I had been left with no money. With money I would have had different choices. In this way my destiny could be mapped out and controlled precisely as he wanted it.

'Can you give me the name of the solicitor?'

'Of course. To be honest, Lena, I'm so glad you found out. I hated not telling you. At first I did it for the money, of course, but I've grown to love you as if you were my own daughter.' She reached out a tentative hand. I let her grasp my hand and squeeze. I didn't blame her. I wasn't angry. All I wanted was to meet Guy again. If he had gone to so much trouble to see that I was safe, he must care for me. I just wanted to tell him that I loved him.

I took a taxi to the solicitor's offices. Mr. Rowberry, a young snazzy junior partner, met me.

'I'm afraid no communication is possible,' he said. 'We have strict instructions not to accept letters or messages from you.'

I blinked in surprise. 'Why?' I whispered.

'He does not want to hear from you,' he said softly. I think he felt sorry for me.

'Can you tell me anything at all about Guy? Is he well?'

He shook his head regretfully. 'I'm afraid I have no authority to discuss your benefactor's affairs at all.'

I stood up.

'Can I buy you dinner?' he blurted out suddenly.

I stared at him. For a flying second it crossed my mind to sit down to dinner with him and try to persuade him to reveal something that would lead me to Guy. And then I looked into his hopeful brown eyes and I shook my head and walked out of the offices.

I felt distraught. There must be a way for me to find him.

It was a beautiful day and a girl wearing a red skirt and a tube top caught my eye. She had a beautiful tattoo of an angel across her chest. Its wings—delicate and incredibly detailed—flowed along her collarbones. Amazing really. She had become a walking canvas. She passed me by and I stood watching her back. She had had a devil tattooed onto it. I watched his snarling face curiously. And then it struck me. That's it. Before she could disappear into the crowd I ran after her.

'Excuse me,' I said.

She stopped and looked at me suspiciously, as if I was about to ask her for money.

I smiled and pointed to her chest. 'Can you tell me where you got your tattoo, please? It's very beautiful.'

She smiled back. 'I got this done in Earl's Court. In a place called Galway City. The artist is called Handsome Mike.'

The taxi dropped me across the street from Galway City. It was a pretty dismal place. A man with purple hair pushed opened the door and entered. I walked across the street and stood at the shop window. It was full of photographs of inked skin. Despite the shabby exterior of his shop, Handsome Mike's work was undeniably delicate and extraordinarily beautiful.

There were pearl necklaces, insects, crosses, devils with horns, mermaids, and a peacock. I stood gazing at the peacock. It was beautifully drawn and colored. There was no doubt Handsome Mike was the person for the job I had in mind.

I opened the door and went inside. It was as dingy inside as it had been outside. Hard to imagine that such a consummate artist worked his magic from here. The man with the purple hair was nowhere to be seen. There were pictures of tattoo motifs all over the walls. The buzzing sound of a tattooing machine stopped and a man wearing a white baseball cap and black rubber gloves came out from a blue door.

'Hello, love,' he greeted.

'Are you Handsome Mike?'

'That I am,' he said, utterly unfazed by the contradiction. Mike was balding, big-nosed, bearded, and more than a little overweight.

'Good. Can you draw me a custom tattoo?'

'Of course. But I don't do traditional; only realism.'

'That's perfect. I want a tattoo of a hawk embracing a seagull. I want the seagull to offer her throat so there is no mistaking her love for the hawk.'

'Yeah sure. Come back tomorrow morning. Say ten o'clock?'

*****

That night I dreamt I was lost in a maze. The maze opened out to a large cold bedroom in a castle. Guy was lying on a bed in his prosthetic mask and dying. Through his mask his eyes were pleading and his lips were calling out to me, 'Come back. Come back to me.'

I woke up and my skin was like ice. I was terrified of losing Guy the way I had lost my brother. I went into the kitchen and made myself a cup of coffee, drank it, and waited for the dawn to slip into the sky.

*****

Even before ten a.m. I was already loitering outside Handsome Mike's place. At ten sharp I entered his shop. He had done the drawing. It was divine. Absolutely incredible.

'I love it,' I said.

'Great. Where do you want it?'

'On my back,' I said, and, turning around, pointed to the area just above my shoulder blades.

He laid me on a bed beside a window. There was a strong lamp overhead. The process took just over an hour. Some bits hurt more than others, but it was bearable. And in the end he held a mirror up to it, and it was exactly as it had been on the paper. The hawk was much bigger than the seagull and it held it within the circle of its wings protectively and lovingly. And the seagull had her throat bared. My left eye twitched. Ready. I was ready.

The interviewer pushed her glasses up her nose and smiled at me. She looked rather pleased with herself. 'Ready when you are,' she said brightly.

'OK.' I shifted on the comfortable chair. A waiter passed, his eyes swiveling in my direction as he walked by. We were doing the interview at a restaurant. There was a glass of cold mineral water on the table. I looked at the lemon stuck between the ice cubes.

'I wanted to use your magazine to pass a message to someone.'

Her eyes widened behind her glasses, the pleased look slipping a notch. 'Ah... This is not the kind of thing we do.'

'I know that, but I will only do this interview if that message can be part of it.'

The pleased look was well and truly gone now. 'It kind of depends what the message is,' she said. 'I can't guarantee anything. It has to pass the editorial review,' she advised cautiously, worriedly.

'The message I want the article to carry can either be included in the body of the article or better still as the title or subtitle.'

'What is it?'

I lifted my hair and, turning away from her, showed her the back of my neck. 'This is the message.'

'It's beautiful,' I heard her say.

I turned back to face her.

'So you just want us to show your tattoo to the world?'

'Yeah.'

'Phew! What a relief. I didn't know what the hell you were going to ask. No problem. This I can definitely do. I'll even get the photographer to take a close-up pic.'

I smiled. 'The photo will need a caption.'

'Yes, it will,' she agreed willingly.

'If the hawk does not come for the seagull at the arch on Valentine's day at four p.m. she will be no more.'

She grinned suddenly. 'Do you know that you've just given me an ass-kicking exclusive?'

I have died every day waiting for you
Darlin' don't be afraid,
I have loved you for a thousand years
I'll love you for a thousand more
—Christina Perri, 'A Thousand Years'
http://bit.ly/1cDvajZ

Chapter 30

Everything that could have gone wrong went wrong that day. And then the taxi got stuck in a jam. It was already three forty-five p.m. I was in such a state. I paid the taxi driver, got out, and ran down Tottenham Court Road. I was gasping for breath by the time I passed Oxford Circus Tube station. If only I had taken the Tube, but it was too late to turn back. A glance at my watch gave me a fright. It was already four oh-five p.m. Shit.

I ran as fast as I could, but there were so many people on Oxford Street. I dodged them as best I could. By the time I reached Marble Arch my lungs were on fire and my legs felt as if they would collapse under me. Four twenty p.m. I looked around, my eyes wildly seeking a tall, dark-haired head. There was no one. I walked to the arch and leaned my aching body against it.

Surely it could not be that he had left after waiting only twenty minutes? It struck me then, painfully, that he had not come at all. He had not read the interview or he had not understood what I meant by 'arch'. He must have forgotten when I told him. It was a great fantasy of mine to meet my lover at Marble Arch. I slumped to the ground, wounded at heart.

I felt so tired I wanted to cry. I hung my head and tried to compose myself. I told myself I would find a different way. I wouldn't give up so easily. I would start to look for castles in England. I would find him no matter what it took.

A pair of shoes came into my line of vision. I swallowed hard. Not daring to hope and yet... It had to be.

Slowly, I raised my head and followed the attached trouser legs. I recognized those strong, muscular thighs. I would know them anywhere in any clothing. My heart was beating so fast I heard it like a drum in my ear. My eyes shot up to his face.

'Happy Valentine's day, baby.'

And I did what I had never done in my whole life.

I fainted.

*****

When I came around I was in the back of a car and lying on his chest. I raised my head and squinted up at him.

'Hello,' he said softly.

I brought my hands up to his face in wonderment. 'My God, your face.'

He smiled, the most amazing smile. 'I've had it repaired...for you. There is still the skin color tattoo to do, but I could not resist your invitation.'

'You are the most beautiful man I have yet seen,' I whispered. 'You are so beautiful, my heart breaks just looking at you.'

I watched his Adam's apple move. There was a look of awe in his eyes. He opened his mouth and then closed it again. 'God!' he breathed. 'How I've missed you.'

I reached up a hand and trailed a finger down the side of his face, caressing his jawbone. His eyes widened.

'OK?' I asked.

'OK,' he said softly.

I took his beautiful face between my hands and our eyes locked. My body began to tingle. His skin was exactly as I had thought it would be. Smoother where it had been worked on and raw silk where it was untouched by fire or surgeons. My breath hitched at the expression in those amazing eyes. Once that was all I'd had to know the man by. Once I had seen him only with my heart. A tear slipped down my face.

He gazed at me, his eyes shiny and dilated. 'You are loved, Lena. You are loved desperately.'

'It's been a long journey to you, Guy.' Another tear escaped and ran quickly down my cheek.

He rubbed it away with his thumb. 'Don't cry, my darling. It's over now.'

I smiled shakily. 'I used to cry for you. At night.'

'I didn't know, my darling. I thought you were repulsed by me.'

'Never. You sent me away before I could tell you that I loved you.'

'I never abandoned you, Lena. Though it might have seemed to you I had. You were always mine. There was not one moment when you ceased to be mine. Not one stray moment when I was not there with you, watching you, protecting you, guiding you back to me. I was always by your side. I was there watching you from the eyes of the woman sitting opposite you on the train, I was there when the man at the end of your carriage followed you safely to your new home. I was there when Roberto told you he suffered from gout, and I was there when the talent scout came to take photographs of you. I was always there, Lena. Always. Cause I am your man. I did everything I could to protect you and keep you safe.'

The truth of his words shone in his eyes.

The familiar smell of his aftershave and the warmth of his skin began to seep into my palms. It was comforting. I wanted to fall into the depths of his eyes. At that moment no one else and nothing else mattered. I was finally safe. I was home.

'I was always yours?'

'Always. You belong to me. From the moment I saw your photo I knew. I fought it and very hard, but it was futile. You are as much one with me as the water that I drink that then becomes part of my blood, my tissue and my sinew. I love you, Lena. You can never know how much. My heart fell to ruin without you.' His voice was husky with emotion.

'We're here,' the driver said, and I was jolted out of that world where there was no one else but Guy and me.

'Where are we?' I asked.

'We're flying home. There's something I want to show you and someone I want you to meet.'

I bit my lip. 'Um, is Misty still working for you?'

'No, I fired her the day after you left.'

'What about Meredith and Tia? Who is taking care of them?'

'Tia died three weeks ago and Meredith died twenty minutes later.'

'Oh, Guy, I'm so sorry.'

'No, don't be sorry. You should have seen Tia before the accident. She was like a puppy. Irrepressible. Boundless energy. Like a bouncing ball. So full of life. That was no life for either them.'

'Will you show me a picture of what she looked like before the accident?'

'Of course.' He took out his wallet, withdrew a picture, and held it out to me.

I took it, looked at it, and gasped.

'What is it?' he asked.

I felt goose pimples rising on my arms. I looked up at him, shocked. 'I've seen her.'

'Tia?'

'Meredith. She was the woman who came out of the mist on the ledge. She told me to hold on. She was going soon. She said she was only waiting for her baby.'

He stared at me and shook his head in wonder. 'That is exactly what she did. She was holding on for Tia.'

'She must have known I loved you and she was giving her blessing to our union.'

He took both my hands in his. 'She also knew I never loved her. I never pretended to, either. I cared about her. That was all. But we both loved Tia.'

I looked again at the picture of the child, how full of life she was, and I remembered the shriveled, hairless creature in the tower and shivered.

'It's over now,' he said.

*****

Even though we arrived at Broughton Castle at night I could see how different it was. Guy had restored it to its former glory. Inside it was beautiful. Mrs. Littlebell started crying when she saw me and Ceba jumped on my chest and nearly tumbled me. Mr. Fellowes smiled at me.

'I'm glad you're back,' he said gruffly.

'There are more staff now, but you can meet them all tomorrow,' Guy said to me. Then he turned to Mr. Fellowes. 'Where is she?'

'In the saloon.'

'Come,' Guy said softly, his hand on the small of my back.

'Who is in the saloon?' I asked, bewildered by all the mystery.

He took me outside the door and turned to me. 'Prepare yourself, she is much changed. I'm sorry, but she is the only one I could find.'

I composed myself and opened the door and there she was. Standing by the piano. Emancipated and haggard beyond her years. Who knows what horrors she had suffered? We stared at each other. Tears began to pour down my face. I brushed them with the backs of my hands.

'Sofia?' I whispered finally.

'Lena,' she called, and though her face was ravaged, her voice was exactly the same. I ran into my Sofia's arms as if I was a child again.

*****

He closed the door to our bedroom and walked toward me.

'I'm really sorry I broke your heart,' he said.

'It's all right. Sometimes it's good to be sad. Anyway, my heart is yours to break. Just don't break it too hard.'

'Oh, my darling, darling. I will never break your heart again. I'd rather gamble my entire fortune away for you. There are so many things I regret in my life. But the one thing I do not regret is buying you. That day when I put you in chains and took you like an animal I spilled my soul into you and became blended with you.'

Our faces began to move toward each other. As if we had done it a thousand times. But we had never kissed. This would be our first kiss. I was barely able to breathe.

Our lips touched. Feather-light.

I felt a shock go through me right down to my toes. It was like diving into an erupting volcano. I was on fire. I opened my mouth and suddenly his hands came around and, grasping me by my upper arms, he almost lifted me off the ground as he pressed me against his hard body. His mouth crashed down on mine; his hand went to my hair.

This was no gentle kiss.

This was the kiss of a starving man who suddenly comes upon a banquet. He sucked my lower lip, he pushed his tongue into my mouth, and, finding my tongue, sucked it into his mouth. He growled even as he claimed my mouth. My knees went weak and I became lost in the most incredible kiss. My heart was racing and between my legs that familiar ache to be filled began again.

He lifted his mouth and looked into my eyes. Desire shone in them.

'Blindfold me,' I said softly.

He shook his head gently. 'Not this time, baby. Let there be nothing between us. This is a joining of our souls.'

I stared at him in the glow of the silk covered lamps. He looked so perfect he was almost unreal. Like a bronze statue of a Greek God.

'You're too beautiful to be real,' he said.

'Funny, I was thinking the exact same thing about you.' I had tried to be light and casual, but my voice had come out sounding shaky and nervous. He was so familiar and yet so foreign.

An expression of sadness crossed his face. 'You're the Beauty here. I am the Beast. I brought you to my castle. Kept you against your will.'

'You were *never* the Beast. You were always my hero.' Gently, I curled my fingers around his gloved hand.

He froze.

'I love you. All of you.' Gazing into his deliberately blank eyes, I slowly removed the glove and looked down at it. There was no other way to describe it. His hand was claw. I raised it to my lips and kissed it as it was the most precious treasure in the world.

He smiled softly and dragged his misshapen thumb along my lower lip. My body's reaction was instantaneous. I felt as if I was on fire. I stepped towards him and pressed myself against his hardness.

'I can feel you trembling,' he said.

'Do whatever you want to me,' I whispered.

'Oh fuck,' he groaned, and closed his eyes for a couple of seconds. 'You make this so hard. I want to be an animal with you. Throw you on the bed and fuck you senseless.'

'Be an animal then.'

'No, not this time. Not after I have raged and wept for you all this time.'

His hands snaked around my body, and lifted me clean off the floor. He laid me on the big bed, and before I knew it my jeans had been tugged off, and my panties were scraping the soles of my feet. He pulled my top over my head and with astonishing expertise unclipped my bra, and threw it behind him. The sheet was cool and silky underneath me. My lips parted. I was waiting.

He stood over me never taking his eyes away from me while he removed his pullover, his jeans, and his black briefs and stood in all his naked glory. I stared at him greedily. I could hardly believe how beautiful he was. He *really* was so toned. So perfect. So erect. And so straight and enormous. My gaze moved back to his eyes and the look in them sent shivers down my spine.

He moved and his knee was between my thighs. I slid down the bed and pushing my clit against the hard bone of his kneecap, ground myself against it with wanton abandon.

'My little wildcat,' he growled, and moved his hand to cup my breast.

'Only with you,' I gasped.

Twin flames leapt into those beautiful eyes. 'God, I want you so much I can hardly control myself.'

I reached up to clasp his neck and his mouth descended on mine. It was not a kiss it was a whirlwind of lust and passion. My tongue was swept up into his mouth and inside his mouth it was sucked on with such intensity and sensuality that I felt as if I was being eaten alive. As if he was feeding off me. I got lost in the delicious sensation of melting and melding with him. The connection became so powerful and fierce that my hips began to writhe involuntarily, pushing into his knee and rubbing desperately against him. When he broke the kiss I stared up at him with wonder. I was breathing hard and my chest heaved. Some sense of loss must have showed on my face.

'You're like a fucking drug,' he muttered.

His touch was delicate but sinuous as his hands brushed down my body to stop on either side of my labia. He spread the fleshy lips wide open and looked down at my opened sex. When our eyes met again, his were dark with desire. He dipped a finger into the swollen wetness.

I cried out.

A second finger followed.

'Yes,' I moaned, as my muscles tightened involuntarily around his fingers. It had been so long, but my body had not forgotten him. It craved him. I craved his cock deep inside me.

 265

'Enter me,' I begged.

He began to finger fuck me with excruciating slowness. My hips lifted off the bed and pushed up against his hand. It was delicious and it was a torture. I did not want my first orgasm after all this time to be at the end of his hand. I tried to hold back.

'Please, I can't take it anymore. Just take me,' I whimpered. I felt almost delirious with need. My head rolled from side to side against the sheet.

'You can take more,' he said, and carried on.

I rose to my elbows and he leaned in and sucked my nipple. My head fell back.

'I don't want to come like this,' I pleaded, hoarsely.

'You won't. I know exactly when to stop,' he murmured as I felt the silky head of his cock push at my entrance. Gently, gently he fitted the thick hardness inside me. And pushed. I had forgotten how big he felt inside. How right and how perfect. For a second I wondered how I had ever survived without him. He paused to allow me to stretch to accommodate him, and the gentleness of the man broke my heart.

'Don't stop,' I cried with longing, pulled in deeper.

And he didn't. He plunged into the very depths of me. So deep I think I lost a little of my sanity. I simply tightened my grip on his shoulders and hung on while he thrust into me like a man possessed, with all the pent up emotion he had stored inside his being. My mind emptied out and became blissfully blank. There was nothing left, but our bodies mating with feral abandon. It was the most beautiful sex we had ever had. So beautiful I cried while he was still inside me.

'Am I hurting you?' he asked with a frown.

'No. Don't stop.'

And then the best part—we came in unison.

Both of us calling each other's names. I could hear the hoarse, wild sounds travelling along the empty corridors and the vast rooms. I clung to his bulky upper-arms and gave in to the little death that transported me to ecstasy.'

*****

I woke up early, Guy's body warm and curled around me. My first thought was that we were fitted together perfectly, like two pieces of a jigsaw. We were made for each other. I sighed softly with happiness. It was almost like a dream. Slowly I turned my head and looked at him in the dim light. His eyes were closed, the dark lashes fanning his cheeks. There were still scars on the sides of his face where the surgeons had grafted on the new skin and the skin itself was a slightly different color, but to me he was the most beautiful thing I had ever laid eyes on. I felt a wellspring of joy burst forth in my being at the thought that he was mine, mine, mine. He belonged to me as much as the blood running in my veins belonged to me.

Very gently I extricated myself out from under his arm and slowly I slid away to the edge of the bed. Noiseless, I sat up. My feet touched the ground before I was suddenly jerked back.

He nuzzled my neck. 'And where do you think you are going at this time of the morning?'

'Oh, darling,' I said. 'This is like a dream come true. I almost can't believe that I am here with you. Sleeping with you.'

'That's all good, but it doesn't answer my question.'

'I was going to the grave. I want to see what you have done.'

'Can't you go later?'

'Nope. I always visit her grave at this time before the sun comes up.' I shrugged. 'I know it sounds funny, but she's never around when the sun is up.'

He looked at me with an expression of great tenderness. 'Don't ever change, Lena. You cannot imagine how innocent and irresistible you are right now.'

'Please don't ever fall out of love with me.'

'Nothing can change the way I feel about you. Don't you know it was dark and lonely in my world until you came? I thought I was dreaming the first time I saw you.' He touched my hair. 'You were so blonde, so white, and so perfect—you looked like an angel. An angel of light. You dazzled me.' He smiled. 'I'm dazzled now.'

But I pushed him off firmly and dressed warmly in a thick knit cream jumper, jeans, and boots. Guy got out of bed and jammed a woolen hat on my head. He wound a long scarf around my neck.

'It's not cold outside,' I protested.

He kissed my nose. 'I love you, Lena Seagull.'

'Keep the bed warm. I'm coming back.'

I turned out of the castle and saw him at the window watching me. He waved and I blew him a kiss. I suddenly remembered the first night I had arrived at the castle, the impression I had of unspeakable loneliness. It was gone. The castle had been purged of its ghosts and renewed and re-energized.

I went over the bridge. It had been repaired and painted. The rocky fields were a riot of wild flowers. The sight of them made my heart sing. I picked a bunch. The cemetery had been cleaned. I went and stood at her tomb. Beside it was the small headstone of her child. They were finally together. I placed the flowers on their graves and felt peaceful and happy. The clouds parted and the sun beamed down and I was caught up in the momentary beauty of the graves, the trees, and the flowers sparkling in the sunlight.

Then I turned back and made my way back to the castle where Guy was waiting for me.

Epilogue

I opened the tall door and, quickly slipping in with Ceba, closed it against the cold, wet wind. I hung up my thick coat and taking a brown towel hanging on a hook briskly rubbed Ceba's underside and legs. We had been to the graveyard and he had run along the river.

Getting down on my haunches next to him, I said in Russian, 'Paw.'

He lifted a paw and I rubbed the muddy pad clean.

'OK, all done,' I said, and putting down his last leg looked into his brown eyes.

He pushed his face closer to mine and I felt his hot breath on my cheek. Without warning he suddenly licked my ear. Laughing, I hugged his big furry neck.

'God, I love you,' I whispered.

That was when he made that sound that he only made when he was alone with me. Like a human baby. I tightened my hold around his neck before I stood up.

'Let's go find Auntie Sofia,' I said, and we walked into the great hall together. I paused in front of the large vase of lilies. They had only fully opened yesterday and their scent was overpowering. I drew their heady perfume in and thought of that sad woman who had appeared out of the mist to urge me to hold on. Lilies had been Meredith's favorite flowers. They were the last invisible connection between Guy and his dead wife. A nostalgia.

One night when we were lying in bed Guy turned to me, and I saw the remnants of a distant pain flickering in his eyes. It made my heart ache for him. Then he told me that he had grown up an orphan trapped in a brutally uncaring and corrupt system where children were commodities. He had run away from its crushing, dehumanizing fist, determined to make it in the big, wide world.

At sixteen he secured the menial job of mailroom boy, but he was so desperate for success that he worked harder and longer than anyone else he knew. He hardly slept and used his meager wages to put himself through night school. It paid off and he began to rise up in the ranks. One afternoon he looked up from his lunch in the café across the road and caught Meredith's eye. She was the boss's daughter.

He was twenty-three and she was thirty-five, but she fell madly in love with him. On his part he was overwhelmed by the sudden grand simplicity of real wealth that she represented. Seen from her privileged eyes his past, with its grinding poverty and humiliation, became as charming an eccentricity as the story of a lord who lost his eye to a tiger in India. And he thought: This is what it means to be truly rich. To be rescued forever from the pettiness of embarrassment. The rich could do anything with impunity.

They got married and she provided the financing for his first business venture. He never looked back for more. The business grew from strength to strength.

'She was my best friend,' he told me, his voice soft and hurt. 'I will never forget what she did for me, or stop being grateful to her. There was only one promise she asked of me.' He blinked. A shadow of a memory no sooner there than gone. 'If ever I wanted someone else I shouldn't go behind her back. I should let her go first. And I kept my promise until you came. Then it was impossible.'

I touched his arm. 'I don't think she would have held that against you. She wanted you to be happy.'

'I know. She was a kind woman.'

I walked away from the lilies toward the Christmas tree—twenty feet tall and filled with twinkling lights and silver decorations. It was magical in its beauty. For some odd reason a vivid memory of Misty laughing as she tied a candy cane to a branch flashed into my mind. How strange I hardly ever thought of her anymore. But the memory brought a dull pain. I had trusted her. Never saw the venom for what it was. Naively I had counted her as a friend. I pushed the pain of her betrayal into a dark recess. Some part of me belonged to her. Just as a part of me belonged to Nikolai, my father, and my mother. I guess we always belong to the people who have hurt us badly, or been badly hurt by us.

As if he felt my sudden sadness, Ceba nuzzled his cold nose into my palm.

'I'm not really sad. That was another lifetime ago,' I told him softly.

We walked away from the tree, and I ran lightly up the stairs, Ceba keeping pace. I knocked on Sofia's door and she called for me to enter.

She was sitting at the window and there was an open book next to her. She smiled at me. She was much changed—so much better than she had looked when I saw her that night more than a year ago—but that well of sadness inside her had never dried. Always I saw it glinting in her eyes. It was months before she spoke about the terrible, terrible things she had suffered. Even now it made my hair stand on end to think of the inhuman things they did to her.

I smiled at her. 'Are you all right?'

'Yes. You've been out walking?'

'It was cold but good.'

She smiled.

I went deeper into the room and knelt in front of her. 'Will you come to the party with us tonight?'

She shook her head.

'Why not? It'll be fun. It's Christmas Eve,' I said enthusiastically.

She lowered her head. 'Next year. Next year, I will be ready.'

I hid my disappointment. 'All right. Promise you will come next year?'

'I promise.'

I leaned forward and kissed her cheek. It smelled faintly of patchouli soap.

Gently, I stroked her hair. She was the last bit of family I had.

'I love you, you know,' she whispered.

'Me too, Sofia. Me too,' I whispered back.

Unshed tears made her eyes glimmer in the leaden light of noon. 'What are you going to wear tonight?'

'I don't know yet. Maybe something black.'

'No, it's the festive season. Why don't you wear your new red dress?'

'OK,' I smiled.

'Good. You look very beautiful in it.'

'I'll come and see you before we leave.'

'Yes, do that,' she said and kissed my cheek softly.

I left her room and went to mine. It didn't take me long to bathe and change into the red dress. I stood in front of the mirror and looked at myself. Sofia was right. It was a lovely dress. I stared into my own eyes. They seemed sad.

When I first arrived back here I used to wake up in a terrible panic. For those few seconds of terror I wasn't sure if I had dreamed it all. That in fact there was no Guy, or Sofia, or Ceba. Then my mind registered the silky tangle of Guy's and my limbs, or his body pressed against mine, warm and solid. And I would reach out a trembling hand and begin to search for his claw. Strangely, it had become agonizingly precious to me, far more than his beautifully repaired face. That claw alone held the memory of his pain and mine.

In the mirror my hands lifted up to brush my hair and I saw the tiny white scar on the inside of my upper arm where the chip had been. Sofia carried the same scar. The sight affected me oddly. Again I lingered on the verge of tears. I brushed my hair slowly, smoothed the red dress over my hips, and slipped into a pair of high heels.

Guy and I had been invited to join the Barringtons for dinner. Blake was old money, from an old banking family, and Lana was just a sweetheart. I didn't know what Guy had told them, but the first time she met me, she walked up to me and enveloped me in her arms. When she pulled away from me she firmly declared, 'We'll be the best of friends, you'll see.' And she was right.

I left the mirror and going to the bed sat on the edge of it and did what I had avoided doing all day. I thought of my father sitting alone in his cold, dusty house eating sunflower seeds, and I wondered why he had done it. What had possessed him to destroy us all so wantonly? Suddenly, Ceba got up and ran down the corridor. At the end of it I heard him jump on Guy and the mad greeting that followed. I stood up slowly and waited.

When Guy appeared at the door the heavy sadness that had followed me all day vanished, and I experienced a rush of pure joy that he was mine. I swallowed the lump in my throat.

His face changed. He came forward with a frown. 'What's the matter?'

'Nothing. I'm just so happy.'

He took me in his arms and we kissed. The kiss was tender and slow, and tears filled my eyes.

He took my chin in his hand. 'What is it, my darling?'

Instantly, I reached for his clawed hand and held it within my hands. 'Nothing. I'm just so happy I've got you.'

He gazed at me intently. 'You might as well tell me now. You'll have to eventually.'

I looked deep into his eyes. Into the warm colors—gold, green, whiskey, all mingling together. Did he know? No, of course he didn't. He just knew that something was different.

'I'm pregnant.'

For some seconds he did nothing. Simply stared at me with a stunned look in those beautiful eyes. And then his powerful arms came around me and suddenly I was lifted up into the air. With a cry of pure delight he began to twirl me round and round until I was laughing and quite dizzy.

'Oh, baby, oh, baby,' he said. He seemed so young. Happier than I had ever seen him. My mind became a camera that snapped pictures of him. Ones that I would treasure forever.

He put me down suddenly, his face watchful. 'Are you happy about it?' he asked. His voice was guarded and almost fearful.

My mouth softened. 'Yes, very.'

'You don't seem very happy.'

'I read that the first thing an abused child will do is to change the balance of power. They will seek to become the abuser. What if I become like my father?' I whispered. I could feel myself begin to tremble.

His face lit up with a huge smile. 'Oh, my darling, darling Lena. That may be true of some, but never of you. Never. You are nothing like your father. There is not a cruel bone in your body. Look at the way you treat Ceba.'

'Do you really believe that?' I asked, but as if by magic the dark clouds were already dissipating.

'You will be a wonderful mother. There is nothing I am more sure of,' he said firmly, and pulled me tight against his body.

I tilted my head up at him and smiled happily. 'Is that an erection you have there, Mr. Hawke?'

He grinned half sheepishly, half wolfish. 'You *are* wearing red.'

'Got a thing for red, huh?'

'And green, and blue, and yellow... Come to think of it, any color would do the trick if you were wrapped up inside it,' he drawled, his thumb stroking over the pulse in my wrist.

'I like that,' I said huskily.

'What, this?' he asked innocently, and lifting my wrist licked it. Hunger flared in his smoky eyes.

'Mmm.' My eyes fluttered closed.

'Whatever you want. All you have to do is ask.'

I opened my eyes. 'If it is a boy, can we call him Niko?'

'Nothing would make me happier.'

And the tears that had threatened to spill, they fell over then. But these were not the tears from this afternoon. These were tears of ecstasy.

He held me close until the tears were spent. 'I love you so much it hurts.'

'Forever?'

He put his hand on my belly. 'Forever. Whatever it is, we will face it together. That much I promise you, Lena Hawke.'

The End

Dear Reader,

Thank you for taking the time to read Guy and Lena's story. They lived in my head until you touched them with your eyes and made them come alive, and for that I will be forever grateful.

xx Georgia

Click on the link below to receive news of my latest releases, fabulous giveaways, and exclusive content.
http://bit.ly/1Oe9WdE

Want To Leave A Review?

No matter how short it may be, it is precious. Please use this link:
http://amzn.to/1Ol1v0m

I **LOVE** hearing from readers so do come and say hello here:
https://www.facebook.com/georgia.lec arre

Sneak preview...

Unlocking her mind...
Will unleash his darkest desires.

Hypnotized

#1 *AMAZON* BESTSELLING AUTHOR
GEORGIA LE CARRE

Hypnotized

Georgia Le Carre

The power of a glance has been so much abused in love stories, that it has come to be disbelieved in. Few people dare now to say that two beings have fallen in love because they have looked at each other. Yet it is in this way that love begins, and in this way only.

−Victor Hugo, *Les Misérables*

Prologue

The girl behind the counter smiled at me and licked her lips. Shit. That was an invitation if ever I saw one. Sorry, honey, I'm married. Hey, I'm not just married, I'm in fucking love. I had the perfect life. A beautiful wife, two little terrors, a successful career. In fact, I was poised to dominate my industry.

The results of my research would soon be made public and I was going to be a star! Life was good.

'Keep the change,' I told her.

Her smile broadened and yet there was disappointment in her eyes.

I grinned and shrugged. 'If I wasn't already hooked I'd ask you out. You're gorgeous.'

'I'm not jealous,' she said flirtatiously.

'My wife is,' I told her, and picked up the tray of drinks: cappuccino for me, latte for my wife, and two hot chocolates for my monsters. Suddenly I heard a man shout, 'Fuck me!' And though those two words had nothing to do with me, my body— No, not just my body, *every part* of me *knew*.

They concerned me.

I whirled around, jaw clenched, still clutching the paper tray of drinks—one cappuccino, one latte, and two hot chocolates—as if it was my last link to normality. For precious seconds I was so stunned, I froze. I could not believe what I was seeing. Then instinct older than life kicked in. The tray dropped from my hand—one cappuccino, one latte, and two hot chocolates—my last link with normality falling away from me forever. I began to race toward the burning car. My car. With my family trapped in it. I could see my babies screaming and banging on the car doors.

'Get out, get out of the fucking car,' I screamed as I ran.

I could see them pulling at the handles, their small spread palms banging desperately on the glass. I could even see their little mouths screaming for me.

'Daddy, Daddy.'

It was shocking how frightened and white their little faces were. I could not see my wife. Where was she?

I was running so fast my legs felt as if they might buckle, but it was as if I was in slow motion. Time had slowed down. At that moment thoughts came into my head at sonic speed, but the disaster carried on in real time. Suddenly my wife lifted her head and I saw her. She was looking out through the window directly at me. I was twenty feet away when I saw everything clearly. I kept on running, but it was like being in a dream where your mother suddenly turns into an elephant.

You don't go *What the fuck?*

You just carry on as normal even though your mother has just turned into a green elephant. I just carried on running. I no longer looked at my children. My gaze was riveted by the sight of my wife. I was ten feet away when the car exploded. Boom! The force of it picked me up and threw me backwards. I flew in the air and landed hard on the tarmac. I did not feel the pain of the impact. I got onto my elbows and watched the fire consume my family and the thick, black smoke that poured from the wreckage.

There was no grief then. Not even horror. It was just shock. And the inability to comprehend. The loss, the carnage, the tragedy, the green elephant. People came to help me up. I was shaking uncontrollably. They thought I was cold so they wrapped me in blankets. They sent me in an ambulance to the hospital. I never spoke. The whole time I was trying to figure out the green elephant. Why? How? It confused me. It destroyed my life, past, present and future.

Two years later
London

Marlow Kane

It is the time you have wasted for your rose that
makes your rose so important.
—Antoine de Saint-Exupéry, *The Little Prince*

'**L**ady Swanson is here for her
appointment,' Beryl said into the intercom.
Even her voice was all at once professional
and terribly impressed.

'Send her in,' I said and rose from my desk.

The door opened and a classically beautiful
woman entered. Her skin was very pale and as
flawless as porcelain. It contrasted greatly
with her shoulder-length dark hair and
intensely blue eyes. Her dress and long coat
were in the same cream material; her shoes
exactly matched the color of her skin. The

overriding impression was of an impossibly wealthy and elegant woman. Women like her lived in movies and magazines. They did not walk into the consulting rooms of disgraced hypnotists.

'Lady Swanson,' I said.

'Dr. Kane,' she murmured.

I winced inwardly. 'Just Marlow, please,' I said and gestured toward the chair.

She came forward and sat. She crossed her legs. They were long and encased in the sheerest tights I had seen in my life. Yes, she was an incredibly polished and cultivated woman.

I smiled.

She smiled back nervously.

'So, I believe you refused to tell Beryl your reason for coming to see me?'

'That is correct.'

'What can I do for you, Lady Swanson?'

'It's not for me. It's for my daughter. Well, she's my stepdaughter, but she is just like my own. I've raised her since she was two years old. She's twenty now.'

I nodded and began to raise the estimation of her age upwards. She must have been at least forty, but she didn't look a day over twenty-eight.

'Her name is Olivia and she met with an accident about a year ago.' Lady Swanson paused for breath. 'She nearly died. She had extensive injuries and was in hospital for many months. When she recovered she had lost her memory. She can remember nothing. She can remember how to do *things*—cook, places—but she cannot remember her past.'

I nodded.

'I was hoping hypnotherapy could help her remember her past.' She leaned forward slightly, her lips parted. 'Do you think you could...hypnotize her?'

I watched her and thought of the men in her life. How easy it must have been for such a beautiful woman to get anything she wanted from a man.

'Lady Swanson, I'm not sure I am the right man for the job. Usually I treat people who want to lose weight, kick a bad habit, or who are afraid of spiders.'

'I understand that, but do you think you could help her, though?'

'To be honest, I've never had such a patient.'

'Well, it's worth a try then?' she pressed hopefully.

'But you have to bear in mind that not everybody can be hypnotized.'

She didn't listen to that. Instead she broke into a smile. It was like the sun shining out from between a crack in a sky full of storm clouds. Yes, she was obviously one of those women who could whistle a chap off a tree, but... I was immune to it. For two years I had wandered around looking for even the smallest spark of the vibrant life that used to course through my veins. All I had ever found was ashes. Even now this beautiful, beautiful woman elicited nothing from me.

'Oh that's wonderful,' she gushed softly. 'You will take her on then?'

I felt almost as if she had subtly manipulated me. 'I'll try. No promises.'

'I did some research on you and your work, and I am certain you are the best person for the job. If anybody can do it, you can.'

I froze at that.

Instantly her face lost some of its glowing enthusiasm. 'I hope you don't think I was snooping into your private affairs? I was only interested in your professional credentials...'

I smiled tightly: the personal stuff came up with the professional stuff. After the accident the two had become inextricably entwined. 'Of course not. It is prudent to check out a practitioner before you go to see him.'

'I just want what is best for my daughter. And you are that. Will you take on her case?'

'Does your stepdaughter know you are here?'

She leaned back and looked out of the window. 'A butterfly wing is a miracle, made up of thousands of tiny, loosely attached pigmented scales that individually catch the light and together create a depth of color and iridescence unmatched elsewhere in nature. Our identities are like the butterfly wing, made up of thousands and thousands of tiny, loosely attached memories. Without them we lose our color and iridescence. Olivia is like a child now. We make all the major decisions for her. The world is a frightening place for her.'

'All right, Beryl will find an appointment for you.'

She smiled. A soft smile. And I had a vision. Her in bed with her shriveled husband. It was not only she who had done a quick Google search. It was not every day that Lady Swanson, of the Swanson dynasty, called my office for an appointment.

For a moment our eyes held and I saw something in hers. Interest. Desire. I let my eyes slide away.

'Thank you... Marlow.'

'Goodbye, Lady Swanson.'

'Ivana, please.'

'Goodbye, Ivana.'

I walked to the door, opened it, and let her out. As she passed me her perfume wafted into my nostrils. Expensive, faint, but still heady. From up close she was even more flawless. I closed the door and walked to my desk. I opened my drawer and taking out a bottle of Jack Daniel's poured myself a huge measure. I knocked it back, swallowed, and closed my eyes. Fuck. Was it ever going to stop hurting? I walked to the window and watched Lady Swanson get into her chauffeur-driven Rolls-Royce Phantom. She stared straight ahead. It was almost as if it was only a dream that she had come into my office and sat in my chair.

The intercom buzzed. 'Can I come in?' Beryl asked.

I sighed. 'Yes.'

The door opened even before I had taken my finger away from the button.

'Well?' she asked, wide-eyed. 'That was a very short first session. What did she want?'

'She wants me to treat her stepdaughter.'

Her eyes became huge. 'What? She wants you to treat Lady Olivia?'

'How did you know that?'

'It was all over the papers. She met with an accident and lost her memory. You have your work cut out for you.'

'Why do you say that?'

'Lady Olivia is known in the tabloids as 'Miss Secretive'. She has never ever given an interview and furiously guards her privacy. There are no pictures of her behaving badly. Ever.' Beryl came deeper into the room and went to my computer. She typed in a few words and turned towards me, her face filled with gossipy excitement, said, 'Here. This is what she looks like.'

I walked toward the computer screen.

It was not a very good picture. A long lens photo. Grainy. And not even in color. But my cock twitched and woke up from its deep sleep.

Coming Soon...

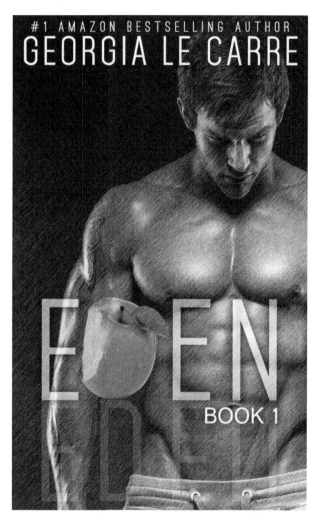

Eden

Synopsis

Haunted by memories of her brother's death, and searching for answers, Lily Hart embarks on a career that takes her into a seedy underworld, where she is exposed to wealth, greed, lust and the reign of gorgeous, powerful, and dangerous men—one man in particular wreaks havoc on her emotions.

At thirty Jake Eden has everything. Looks to die for, money, power and a never-ending line of twisted, fucked-up women willing to do anything to get with him. Love? Love was for pussies…until a woman with the stage name of 'Jewel' arrives on the scene. She alone is different from all the others.

Oozing pure, unadulterated sex, strong, intelligent and independent, she is everything he should keep away from, but she makes him itch to tame her and keep her for himself.

Her lure is addictive and undeniable and soon he is hooked.

But when the line between betrayal and loyalty is put to test…

Will love be stronger than revenge?

Printed in Great Britain
by Amazon

26469691R00172